W9-BQT-289

THE SLEDDING HILL

Other books by Chris Crutcher

Whale Talk

Ironman

Staying Fat for Sarah Byrnes

Athletic Shorts

Chinese Handcuffs

The Crazy Horse Electric Game

Stotan!

Running Loose

King of the Mild Frontier:
An Ill-Advised Autobiography

Greenwillow Books
An Imprint of HarperCollins*Publishers*

THE SLEDDING HILL

CHRIS CRUTCHER

This book is a work of fiction. References to real people, events, establishments, organizations, or locales are intended only to provide a sense of authenticity, and are used to advance the fictional narrative. All other characters, and all incidents and dialogue, are drawn from the author's imagination and are not to be construed as real.

Printed in the United States of America. For information address HarperCollins Children's Books, a division of HarperCollins Publishers, 1350 Avenue of the Americas, New York, NY 10019.
www.harperchildrens.com

The text of this book is set in Adobe Garamond.
Book design by Chad W. Beckerman

Library of Congress Cataloging-in-Publication Data
Crutcher, Chris.
The sledding hill / by Chris Crutcher.
p. cm.
"Greenwillow Books."
Summary: Billy, recently deceased, keeps an eye on his best friend, fourteen-year-old Eddie, who has added to his home and school problems by becoming mute, and helps him stand up to a conservative minister and English teacher who is orchestrating a censorship challenge.
ISBN 0-06-050243-6 (trade).
ISBN 0-06-050244-4 (lib. bdg.)
[1. Death—Fiction. 2. Future life—Fiction. 3. Censorship—Fiction. 4. Elective mutism—Fiction. 5. High schools—Fiction. 6. Schools—Fiction. 7. Idaho—Fiction.] I. Title.
PZ7.C89S1 2005 [Fic]—dc22 2004020098

First Edition 10 9 8 7 6

IN MEMORY OF ZACH CLIFTON,
WHO SPOKE WHALE TALK

CONTENTS

I

Death Does Not Take a Holiday

When we were in grade school most kids thought Eddie Proffit was stupid because he would ask questions no one else would think of. It's human nature to think if you weren't the person to think of something, it must be dumb. But Eddie knows things.

I was Billy Bartholomew, smartest kid in class; arguably smartest in school, which was supposed to be a minor miracle because my father is the school janitor. It is also human nature to define a person by his or her job, which is a mistake when it comes to my dad. He doesn't have a huge drive to get rich, so he's considered ordinary. At any rate, I was supposed to grow up and rattle the world, and Eddie was supposed to grow up and run his father's gas station. Everyone thought our friendship was odd; what was a smart kid like me doing hanging out with a kid with an IQ short of triple digits? Truth is, Eddie's IQ turned out to be off the charts. His mind bounces from one thing to the other pretty much however it wants, though, and long before he should be finishing up one thought, he's on to something else. Eddie doesn't come to very many conclusions.

In fifth grade, when my dad discovered Eddie scored sixty-five on his IQ test, he asked Eddie what happened, because Dad knew that couldn't be right.

"I was answering the questions," Eddie said, "and then I started seeing what a neat pattern I was making filling in those little ovals, and before I knew it I was making neater and neater patterns."

"You weren't even reading the questions?"

"I wasn't even keeping it to one answer per row," Eddie told him. "Did you see my answer sheet? It looks way cool."

So my dad went to the principal, who was about to put Eddie in special ed for every class but PE, and told her she can't do that. "He scored a *sixty-five*," my dad said, "without reading the questions."

The principal was all into protocol and all out of taking advice from the school janitor and wouldn't let Eddie retake the test. But Dad had a key to every room and file drawer in school, so he found a test, took Eddie to the furnace room, and had him answer the questions five at a time. Eddie added almost a hundred points to his IQ that afternoon. When the principal told Dad he was out of line, Dad took the test over to the Chevron station to bring Eddie's dad up to speed.

Eddie didn't attend any special ed classes.

The principal went ahead and recorded the

sixty-five IQ on his permanent record anyway and no one knew the story of the second test, so it was generally thought I did Eddie's homework for him when he started to get good grades. I didn't do one of his assignments. He would go to the furnace room for an hour and a half after school every day, and my dad would break up his homework with little jobs to keep him focused, and Eddie did great. But he continued to ask strange questions and challenge teachers when they said something he thought couldn't be true, and he was pretty much considered a pain in the neck.

Eddie and I used to run everywhere. We'd been winning the annual Fourth of July races as long as we could remember and had decided when we got into high school we'd be the heart of a stellar cross-country team. We were both too skinny to play football, and in a high school this small it is not considered cool to go sportless, so cross-country was it.

So it's early summer, five days after Eddie's fourteenth birthday, and he's getting ready to bike out to the hot springs with me to spend the afternoon swimming and rolling in the warm mud. Eddie's been working four hours a day, eight to noon, at his dad's service station, the last full-service gas station in the solar system, to hear Mr. Proffit tell it. It may not be the last one in the solar system, but it's definitely the last in Bear Creek, population 3,065, situated high in the Idaho panhandle, a few miles from the Canadian border. Anyway, Eddie has been helping his dad fix truck tires all morning and is ready to hit the warm water.

Bear Creek is a mess. Duffy Reed Construction has been hired to widen Main Street. They've got the pavement dug out from city limit to city limit along with another two feet of dirt below that, so if you step off the sidewalk without looking you could take a serious header. Proffit's Chevron, which Eddie's dad used to call Non-Proffit's Chevron, is the only place in town that fixes truck and heavy-equipment tires, and Mr. Proffit has been doing just that twelve hours a day—four hours with Eddie's help and eight by himself—to keep up with Duffy Reed's sharp-rock punctures.

He's got it down to a science. Air up four tires at a time to find the leaks, let the air out, break them down, remove the tubes if they have them, patch them, throw them back together, air them up, and roll them to the rack out back so the next driver with a flat can replace it with a repaired one and roar out in under six minutes. Four at a time. John Proffit's a tire-fixin' fool.

That day Eddie's dad stops only once to have lunch with Eddie's mom—her name is Evelyn—and he's back to fixing tires, somewhat disgruntled and distracted because he got chicken salad instead of tuna, and he forgets to let the air out of one of the tires before breaking it down.

Eddie's mom catches Eddie and me just as we're about to head out to the hot springs, and she gives

Eddie a monster hunk of chocolate cake and some milk in a thermos to take to his dad.

But his dad is lying in the middle of the wash bay next to an exploded truck tire, nose plastered onto the side of his cheek like he was maybe painted by Picasso, his blood trickling into the drain, deader than a doornail. No chocolate cake and milk for John Proffit today.

Eddie stands there staring. This *can't* be. His dad has told him eight jillion times how dangerous the lock ring on a truck wheel is. You *always* make sure the air pressure is zero before breaking it down. When it's repaired you place it inside the wire cage before airing it up or, in the absence of a cage, turn it facedown on the concrete. If the lock ring isn't locked, it might just as well be a bomb. It will take your head right off your body. Eddie knows that as well as he knows to brush his teeth before bedtime. "It'll take your head right off your body, buddy." Eight jillion times.

I'm waiting outside by the gas pumps, so Eddie

just walks back and gets on his bike and we pedal off to the hot springs. He doesn't tell me what happened because he knows it isn't real. He's had dreams like this; not about truck tires, maybe, but dreams where you come home to find the house empty and no sign of your parents. Shoot, even *I* used to have that dream. It freaks you, but when you finally wake up, there they are.

"Hey, man," I say when we've pedaled about a mile, "hear those sirens? Let's go back and see what it is."

"Naw," Eddie says. "Probably just Mrs. Madden set her hamburgers on fire again."

I'm easy to convince. We've been planning to bike to the hot springs for a week.

Flash forward three weeks. I'm trying to hook up with Eddie to hang out or bike back out to the hot springs. I have been way cool, doing everything I can to help Eddie back to his regular life after his dad was suddenly gone and his mom's brain got kidnapped by the Red Brick Church. Since the day his dad died, ask Evelyn Proffit any question and the answer will include God's Plan, which, by the way, you seldom hear about unless something awful happens or one person escapes death in a situation where nobody else did. Eddie's been attending church with her Wednesday nights and Sundays, but it doesn't help much. For one thing, he can't keep his mind on Reverend Tarter's sermons for more than thirty seconds at a time, and for another, he's mad at God. Eddie figures if God's Plan included his dad taking a bite out of an exploding lock ring, well, God can plant a big one on Eddie's keister. Also, he ran out in the middle of his dad's funeral and the Red Brick Church people have taken to treating him like one of the lepers to which the Reverend Tarter so fondly refers in every third sermon.

I was one of those dweebs who loved having information other people didn't care about, so I hated it when Eddie got thrown out of class for talking out of turn or for not stopping after the fifth or sixth time the teacher said, "That's enough, Eddie." On his worst days he spent more time in the office than in class. I loved how he'd just tell a teacher she was wrong or ask questions at a machine-gun clip without raising his hand if she said something he thought was suspect. So I started working with him on ways to stay in class. Once we pooled our money and bought one of those electronic dog collars you can use to shock the dog by remote if he starts to pee in a corner of the living room or tears after a mother pushing a baby stroller. Eddie wore the collar on his ankle and sat directly in front of me in class. Every time I'd see him start to speak out of turn or do something that clearly indicated he was fixin' to make an unplanned exit, I'd give him a jolt. Most of the time it worked, but if I didn't catch him before he blurted, he'd get out about three words and a scream as the shock hit him. The idea was solid in theory, problematic in execution.

Then I started noticing when we'd ride our bikes, Eddie could stay on any subject, and the harder we rode the more focused he was. Since we both liked to run and bike, I started holding most of my important conversations with him on the move, and he seemed like a way different kid. I tried to tell our teacher that if she'd just let him pace the perimeter of the room at an accelerated gait, he'd be the smartest kid in class. Again, easy theory to formulate, harder to sell.

Eddie discovered I was right, though, and started running and biking everywhere he went, whether I was with him or not, which created a demand for deodorant until he started carrying fresh clothes in a backpack and people got used to him showering at their houses whenever he came to visit. The more he exercised, the calmer he got.

So, biking is what Eddie is doing while I'm trying

to catch up with him on this day, and when I can't find him I realize I'm so bored I might as well go help my dad with summer maintenance on the gym up at the high school. Only Dad's out running an errand, and for some reason that really hacks me off and (this was a *real* lapse) I kick a stack of Sheetrock leaning precariously against the stage and turn around to stomp out. The operative word in that last sentence is "precariously." Four of the sheets fall forward as I walk away, and the upper edge catches me at the base of the skull, knocks me down, and snaps my spine.

Guess who finds me.

Around noon, after a ten-mile bike ride to the radar site on West Mountain, during which he has some choice words with God about who goes and who stays on this stupid planet, Eddie pedals over to my place. My dad is eating lunch and says if Eddie will run up to the school to see if I'm there, he'll feed us, which sounds to Eddie like a better plan than lunch with his mother because he's really hungry from riding so hard and at his house saying grace now takes longer than consuming the meal and turns into a way bigger deal than simply asking God to make sure the food isn't full of botulism. Eddie whips up to the school and there I am; only we have had our last lunch.

He can't lift the Sheetrock high enough to get me out, but he does get me turned over partway, and sees what you could only call a ghastly expression on my face.

Let it never be said that Eddie Proffit doesn't know what to do when he finds a dead body. He pedals straight out to the hot springs, sheds his clothes, and buries himself in the warm mud right up to his neck and sits there the rest of the afternoon, trying to make what he's just seen into a fantasy, like he was able to do with his dad for a few hours before his world caved in on itself.

Only he can't pull it off; he has recently had the

experience of it not working and because his mind is bouncing like a Super Ball in a racquetball court. So he rinses off and pedals back to my house, because one thought that finally scoots across his brain is, he better tell my dad. Of course by that time the whole town is humming with the news and half of it is looking for Eddie, because my dad told them he must have seen me because of how the Sheetrock was moved. What a guy. In the middle of his crippling hurt, he thinks of Eddie.

Eddie is seriously glazed over. Rollie Mount, the county sheriff, catches up with him riding down the mess that is Main Street, loads his bike into the trunk, and drives him home, where Eddie doesn't want to go because he's afraid of what he might say if his mother mentions God's Plan. But Mrs. Proffit is out looking for him, so Rollie stays.

Rollie says, "Hey, man, I know you're messed up, but I have to ask a few questions."

Eddie nods.

"You found Billy, right? Under the Sheetrock?"

Eddie nods again.

"Did you try to pull him out?"

Another nod.

Rollie takes a deep breath. "Was he still alive, when you were trying to pull him out?"

Eddie's mind explodes. He never thought of that. What if *he* killed me, trying to get me out from under all that? He opens his mouth to speak, but the answer weighs on his chest like an anvil and suddenly he can barely breathe. Coherent thoughts won't form, and his mind spins. It will be awhile before anyone hears another word from Eddie Proffit.

2

Life after Life

When you first die, you don't know you're dead. You know something is *way* different, but you've been playing the game with such intensity, it's hard to realize you've just stepped out of it. The good news is, there's no pain. First I'm pinned to the floor and there is no physical sensation except I can't move, and then I look to a spot on the floor right beside me and suddenly I'm at that spot looking back at a seriously expired Billy Bartholomew, and I'm thinking,

Dang! That was dumb. I'm on the bleachers by the time Eddie finds me, and I try to holler at him before remembering that when you weigh only twenty-one grams—the difference between the weight of a live body and that same body croaked—you have no room for a voice box. So I watch and root for him as he tries to pry my body from under the Sheetrock, which is just too heavy. And I think, Eddie just went into a *dark* room in his Earthgame; two important guys dead in one month, and he found them both. And then he is out of the gym and out to the hot springs, and I keep trying to get his attention to let him know it's okay, but I don't remember how to do that yet.

The longer you're dead, the clearer you become about what the deal is: that your Earth life, which lasted what seemed like a long fourteen years, was not even a subatomic blip in eternal time, and that you just hit TILT! You also remember instantly that emotions are for the living and you don't need them anymore, and in fact they aren't available. There is huge joy—not the emotion of happiness, but the pure joy of *knowledge*—and a sense of coming home. The knowledge itself is monstrous, huge and expanding at warp speed, and you laugh in wonder at all the crazy considerations you had while playing the Earthgame because you were so focused you thought things were important. You immediately understand what the *Don't Sweat the Small Stuff* book was about. You know that in the blink of an eye to the minus one billionth, universe time, when all your friends will also be dead, you can bump into any one of them you want to, so even if you could feel emotion, it wouldn't be sadness.

I could take right off, but once I see my friend struggling so hard to get my abandoned body out from under all that weight, then fleeing to the hot springs, curiosity and my sense of connection to him draws me to stay. I wonder if I can help; not to get my body free, but to deal with what seems to him like a hurricane of calamity in his life. He looks *so* freaked out.

So I hang around a second, universe time.

In case you think that's some big sacrifice, you should know that once you're dead again—which is like being truly alive—you can haul yourself around eternity at soul-boggling speeds. Earth scientists consider the speed of light to be the ultimate speed. We travel at the speed of *imagination*. Light speed is to imagination speed as the forming of the Grand Canyon is to NASCAR. Times a zillion. Hard to explain in the relative language of Earth. You have to be here. The point is, I can hang around a second and at the same time whip back and forth rediscovering the knowledge of eternity, which I left at the doorstep when I entered Earth. You did, too. So did Eddie Proffit. But the unique thing about Eddie is, he brings the ghost of a memory for his life before life to his Earthgame. That's the good news and the bad news—more accurately, the advantage and the challenge—for him, because while it gives him incredible insight, it also makes him touchy, as in sensitive, and his bouncing brain doesn't allow him to focus on any one thing for too long. Eddie can light on a truth and be gone before he ever knows he was there. What I know now that I'm dead is that there is a microminisecond when his brain is in mid bounce, when I can bump him.

Two dead bodies in a month. Both loved ones. That much loss can take out the best of us. If you had seen the desperation on his face, the *intent*, while he was trying to get me out from under that Sheetrock, and felt the pounding of his heart while he was buried in the mud at the hot springs, you'd know why I'm going to watch a second, universe time.

Eddie sees right away that a big advantage to falling silent is that you get to stop explaining yourself. You're allowed a period of grace if the condition seems to have sprung from the violent deaths of your father and your best friend, and that period of grace gives you a head start into a later time when adults in charge and other detractors decide you have grieved long enough and it's time to speak up.

There are disadvantages as well. Over a relatively short period Eddie irritates virtually everyone with reason to communicate with him. Also he goes without certain luxuries—like the feather-light, iron-tough pair of New Balance running shoes at Bowlden's Sporting Goods, or the four-pound butter horn in the window of Stiburk's Bakery—and even a few necessities, because staring longingly at something you want might just make those capable of giving it to you, *not* give it just to see if they can make you talk. Eddie accustoms himself to a certain level of deprivation.

In the end, the advantages outweigh the disadvantages. For one thing, while irritating certain people may fall into the negative column, irritating others, such as the Reverend Sanford Tarter, is most definitely a plus. Eddie and I have been anticipating Tarter in our lives for some time, with significant trepidation. The reverend is a fire-and-brimstone, eye-for-an-eye kind of preacher who can make a simple thing such as being a sinner seem like taking center stage in a Stephen King novel. Under normal circumstances a sinner could avoid him by simply staying away from his church, but he's also one of three Bear Creek High School English teachers, so unless you drop out of school after junior high to work in the lumber mill, he'll get his hands on you.

You start hearing about Tarter around fifth grade, and the day you hear about him is a good day to start worrying. He is the king of creative discipline. Somehow he has cleared with the school board certain techniques of torment, such as requiring student insurgents to stand before the class with their arms extended to the sides, like a crucifixion without the cross, or sit with their backs against the wall as if in a chair, without benefit of that chair. He calls these "stress" positions, and they are evidently perfect to assume when you need to think about what you've done wrong, like chewing gum or talking out of turn or trying to get the attention of a friend when you're bored almost blind.

Eddie has many reasons for wishing his dad was still around, but a big one right now would be to insulate him from Tarter. They were exact opposites; Tarter is five-six and weighs 132 pounds and John Proffit was six-five and weighed 231. (*That's* a little coincidence only I, from my privileged vantage point, know.) Eddie's mom and dad were very different in their religious beliefs, Mrs. Proffit far more traditional and "fundamental" in her quiet way, and Mr. Proffit a believer only in what he could see and touch. Mrs. Proffit attended church religiously—pun intended—and Mr. Proffit attended on Christmas and Easter to hear his wife sing in the choir. Eddie started going to Sunday school in first grade because that was prerequisite for Friday night roller skating in the church basement. I went, too, to protect him, because when your mind wanders the way Eddie's does, skating on a crowded roller rink is classified under "danger to self and others."

Sunday school is where Eddie first ran afoul of Tarter.

His first difficulty came when we were eight. Mr. Foster was our Sunday school teacher, and he had just told us the Old Testament story of Jonah living in the belly of a whale. The way Eddie's mind works, when he hears some great story like that he has to picture it, imagine what it would really be like. He'd seen *Pinocchio*, and Pinocchio also spent time in the digestive tract of a fish, so he could see how a cartoon character could pull it off, but the Question Man inside him, the Man Who Seeks the Truth No Matter the Consequence, told him if you were a real human inside a real whale it would be seriously dark and you'd be working your way through all kinds of slime if you were looking for a way out, which you most certainly would be.

"What kind of protective rain gear did Jonah have?" Eddie asked.

We all looked up.

"Excuse me?" Foster said. Foster ran Three Forks Auto Parts and volunteered reluctantly as a Sunday school teacher.

"My dad told me the digestive juices in a human stomach are strong enough to dissolve a jawbreaker like a sugar cube in hot water," Eddie said. "A whale's gotta have at least as strong digestive juices as us, right? And if Jonah's in there wearing his regular Bible clothes, it seems like they'd get, like, seriously eaten up. So I thought he must've had some kind of special rain gear or something."

"God was taking care of Jonah," Mr. Foster said.

"I know," Eddie said back. "That's what you said. So did he give him a special suit? Or did he just make the whale's stomach acids not work? That's no fair to the whale. I mean, even if he's gonna spit Jonah up whole in a day or two, there has to be a bunch of other stuff down there he needs to digest. I mean, whales just suck in everything. You know—"

Eddie stopped because I put my hand over his mouth.

"Eddie, being a true Christian is about having faith. It is disrespectful to question lessons from the Bible. What you hear in this room is true."

Eddie gave a muffled okay, because I wouldn't take my hand away. I could see by the marble popping up at the top of Foster's jaw that Eddie was close to trouble, which happened often when he went ahead and said what he was thinking.

But when your mind bounces like Eddie's, it's easy to forget what you've been told, and a couple of weeks later, when we were hearing about Moses allegedly parting the Red Sea to help his people get out of Egypt, Eddie started wondering about the sea life on the bottom.

"I could see how the fish could just swim off to the side and stay where the water is," he said, "but what about the crustaceans and stuff that lived on the bottom? It had to take a while for the Israel guys to get across, right? I mean, it's a sea, not just like a small lake. Wouldn't the animals that lived on the bottom dry up or drown in the air?"

"God takes care of all his creatures," Foster said, and Eddie could see the marble growing again, but when you're Eddie you get pretty used to being in trouble, especially in places where you're supposed to be quiet or speak one at a time, so being in trouble isn't an abnormal or distressing circumstance.

"Yeah, I know you said he takes care of all his creatures—and I won't even count the chipmunk my mom killed in the car on the way to school Friday—but did he move them over so they could still be under the water, or did he just make it okay for them to be dry?" And before Foster could answer: "Oh, he would of moved them over, or all those Israel guys would be stepping on them." And before I could get my hand over his mouth: "'Course that would give them a lot better traction."

Foster was up and out of the room, and the next face we saw was Tarter's and we got to see some biblical *wrath*, because now *Eddie* was up and out of the room and his feet didn't touch the floor once. I couldn't hear exactly what Tarter said to him, but I did hear the word "blaspheme" four times. I got anxious for class to be over so I could see if Tarter had disappeared Eddie. He hadn't, but he sure made him stand with his arms out for a long time.

Mr. Foster began sending Eddie to a wooden bench in the hall when he got tired of not answering his questions adequately. Eddie was grateful for the bench, because it was a lot easier to sit there than it was to stand in the outer alcove with his arms extended. Between the bench and my hand over his mouth, that was the last time we saw Tarter that mad for a while, though Tarter stopped us a week later as we were leaving the Sunday school and asked Eddie if his dad was putting him up to this.

Eddie said, "Up to what?"

"All the foolish questions."

"I thought you said there was no such thing as a foolish question."

"Your dad *is* putting you up to this."

Eddie shook his head, incensed because he resented that Tarter thought he wasn't smart enough to come up with his own foolish questions. In truth, Tarter would rather they came from Eddie than Mr. Proffit, because Eddie's dad was the smartest gas station owner in five states and Tarter couldn't make him stand with his arms out like he could with Eddie.

3

Billy Bartholomew aka Freddy Krueger

For a while, right after all the dying, it seems to Eddie like it's All Tarter, All the Time. He's going to church with his mother because, well, because she makes it hard to refuse. Without benefit of speech, it's tedious to come up with an excuse, so he listens to her sing and lets his mind wander.

He listens in short spurts to Reverend Tarter's words and imagines his father arguing with him down by the gas pumps, and he starts smiling and sometimes giggling, which is right about the time he gets his mother's elbow in his ribs.

Once school starts he'll have Tarter as a teacher every day, as a preacher on Wednesdays and Sundays, *and* Tarter has started coming to his house two or three times a week to help Eddie's mom with her "grieving process." *That* doesn't feel quite right, because often he stays for dinner and sits where Eddie's dad once sat. It is not a good way for Eddie to spend dinnertime, particularly with Tarter urging him to consider what his silence is doing to his mother, to rejoin the world, which he never really unjoined; he just reduced his participation. Eddie isn't talking, so he can't say that, and Tarter rambles, undeterred. Eddie continues to imagine his father answering.

It would be hard to articulate how much Eddie misses his dad. Before my dad started helping him, if it hadn't been for *his* dad, Eddie would have accepted the mantle of dumbest kid in our class. Most of his schoolwork indicated that his parents should have thrown him back. But Mr. Proffit's brain was the prototype for Eddie's, so he taught him to deal with it. "When teachers say you have a disorder," Eddie's dad told him, "they're full of it. Your mind just works differently. Most kids dwell on one thing at a time, which is usually whatever boring thing the teacher is talking about. You pick the parts that have the power to hold your attention, and when they aren't interesting anymore, you move on, like anyone who doesn't want to die of boredom should. And besides, listen to you," he went on. "You and Billy sound like a couple of English profs."

Any time Eddie came home crying, once again in trouble for not paying attention or for speaking out of turn, his dad told him not to worry; that he'd be an astronaut while the rest of us were balancing other people's taxes or selling insurance or teaching school. Then they'd retire to the backyard and find the North Star or the Big Dipper or Orion's Belt, and Eddie would pay attention just fine.

Eddie does not like looking to the head of his kitchen table at the Reverend Tarter instead of his dad.

I've been dead a good two months, Earth time; Eddie no longer visualizes my coffin as it disappears into that dark hole (believe me, *I* didn't go there with my body that *could* be feeding worms and mud varmints but instead is filled with formaldehyde and stuffed into an airtight box so it can do *no* environmental good), no longer automatically wonders what I'd say about the latest Seattle Mariner trade or whether Montana West is the craziest girl in school.

And then he closes his eyes one night and there I am, all dead and stuff, staring at him exactly like I was the day he tried to turn me over. When I get his full attention, I *smile*. If he weren't so freaked out, he'd want to know what I think I have to smile about, but he *is* freaked out and pops awake like he's spring-loaded. And there I am, framed in his bedroom window, staring through the blackness, and he leaps up and pulls the drapes, except he knows I've found my way into his closet, because he can *hear* me there! And he flips on the light and jerks open the closet door, but the noise is suddenly behind him in the big storage closet on the other side of the room, so he jerks *that* door open, and it is seriously dark in there. If he wants light, he has to walk a good ten feet into the darkness and screw in the lightbulb, which there is *no* chance of his doing, so he slams the door and sits on his bed with the lights on, sweating like he's going to melt.

Now, you gotta know it isn't really *me*. I might try to scare Eddie into the next time zone if I were alive, but scaring him while I'm dead could get him a mental-health diagnosis.

His mother hears the closet door slam and hollers up from her bedroom, though she knows he won't answer because mute guys, by definition, don't answer, and he flips out the light and crawls *way* under the covers, because he wants her to think he's asleep if she comes up and he wants me to think he's *gone* in case she doesn't.

After that night Eddie thinks he's going stark raving mad, and if I weren't privy to information the living aren't, I might have thought that, too. In his mind, I'm everywhere. Mrs. Proffit opened the service station again because "We have to eat," and while she's filling the tank and checking the oil in some customer's car, Eddie washes the windows all the way around, and guess whose face fills up the back one, looking the same, all dead and smiling. (I didn't look *that* bad the day he found me.) He sees me in stores. Out at the hot springs. I almost scare him into talking, but he doesn't know who to tell.

It comes to a head on a Wednesday night. Mrs. Proffit is ready for church, and Eddie sits on the couch watching TV. She is getting better at decoding his style of communication, such as it is, understanding that if he doesn't move once she's ready, he's probably not going unless she makes it a big deal.

He doesn't imagine his mom would be much help should I decide to suck his blood or scoop out his eyeballs with a spoon, but there's comfort in having somebody—anybody—in the house when you're under ghostly siege, and his mom isn't gone more than fifteen minutes before he wishes he'd gone with her. But it's too late, so he turns on every light in the downstairs part of the house, microwaves a bag of Paul Newman's buttered popcorn, turns on the TV, loud, and wraps himself in a blanket on the couch.

Wind whistles through the branches on the large pine tree next to the house, and fat raindrops begin splattering against the windows. In the distance, thunder rumbles. The sky lights up, and he throws off the blanket and scurries around the living room, pulling the drapes. The last thing he needs is theatrical lighting behind my smiling dead head, should I make an appearance.

I said before, when you're dead there are a few people you can *bump,* and Eddie is a prime candidate.

But you can't bump them just anytime, because you weigh twenty-one grams and you are feathery. You are subtle. You need an *in*. I would give Eddie a big break right here, but he gives me no *in*. He is busy being deranged, which clogs all his avenues.

He flips to the Discovery Channel because how bad could *that* be, and that's exactly what he finds out. The Discovery Channel has discovered a real live haunted house. A woman in a small town in Massachusetts was murdered in this house generations ago. The police never solved her murder, but at certain times the current occupants encounter what looks like a stain on the wall but turns out to be the ghostly outline of the victim, screaming. The stain is brownish red and if whoever sees it summons the courage to *touch* it—like why would they? Eddie wonders, but they do—it feels wet. Now while this might be, given his current emotional state, a good time to see if he can find Lassie on the Animal Channel, he can't pry his gaze from the screen. A family member will be minding their business and the stain appears behind them and they turn around and see it and Eddie pulls the blanket over his head and then, like a soldier calling in friendly fire, makes a sight tunnel and keeps right on watching for the next victim. Outside, the wind howls and rain slaps against the windowpanes like running soles on wet pavement.

Some totally irrational voice tells him he can scare me out of his head with the likes of *this*. It's like with forest fires, he thinks. Firefighters create a controlled fire around the uncontrolled fire to stop it from spreading. It makes a certain kind of sense, because even though the story on the Discovery Channel is supposed to be real (it is only about 6.3337 percent accurate), the family members are actors and the face, though big-time scary, lacks the power of being a real live dead person, unlike yours truly. Eddie pulls the blanket tighter. A girl, the youngest daughter, stands at the kitchen counter making a peanut-butter sandwich. She is alone, and behind her the shadowy stain begins to form. The low, dark music builds, and if Eddie were talking he'd scream at her, but he's not, and the stain becomes more and more pronounced. The girl pats the top of the sandwich as violin strings increase to a scream and—

CRACK! A bolt of lightning flashes so close to Eddie's house that deafening thunder roars simultaneously and the room goes black. Eddie screams, because that's not exactly talking and he couldn't help it if it were. His heart hammers against his chest as he hyperventilates like an industrial-strength respirator. It's darker than a bat cave (which is blindingly bright compared to a black hole, but Eddie doesn't have a black hole to compare with), and he's *sure* something's going to grab him, so he throws off the blanket and leaps up, whirling in the middle of the living-room rug like a kickboxer, sensing fingers millimeters from his neck.

Above the beating rain and the howling wind, a

voice in his head says, Turn into the slide. (I swear it isn't me.)

He freezes; listens: *Turn into the slide.*

On a Saturday afternoon the winter before he died, Eddie's dad took Eddie behind the service station to teach him to drive his pickup on ice. It would be several years before Eddie was eligible for his license, but Mr. Proffit liked to stay ahead of the game with important things, wanted Eddie ready for the tough challenges. Eddie's dad pushed the seat all the way back, let Eddie sit between his legs so Eddie could operate the steering wheel while he operated the brakes (and take over the wheel if the situation called for it). Mr. Proffit put them into slide after slide. "Everything in you will tell you to turn the wheel away from the direction of the slide," Mr. Proffit said before the first try, "but that will just throw you further out of control. Trust me."

Easier said than done. His dad was right. *Every*thing in Eddie said turn away, and he did and they slid across the back lot, time after time. But eventually Eddie got the hang of it, and finally his dad hit the brakes and Eddie turned into it and lo and behold the pickup straightened out. To Eddie it seemed like saying "yes" while shaking his head no, but there was a *free* feeling to it, like he'd tricked the universe, or at least discovered one of its minor secrets, which, in fact, he had.

That is the feeling Eddie now seeks, and the voice is telling him to go in exactly the wrong direction to make things right.

He feels his way along the wall to the kitchen, slowly past the table, the stove, the fridge, to the closed door to the stairway leading to the cold, unfinished basement. He steps through, pulls it shut, grips the handrail like a lifeline, and moves slowly into the pitch black.

It's been weeks since Eddie first saw me dead, and he is sick to death of being scared; so sick he's willing to give up and die to escape the dread, or at least thinks he is. At the bottom of the stairs he releases the handrail, moves to the middle of the room, and sits on the cold concrete. If you're coming for me, Billy B., he thinks, just do it. He hears himself sobbing, but he will sit here in the middle of the basement floor in pitch black until something gets him or until he's not scared anymore. He trembles and sobs, and he waits, past the embarrassment of being newly fourteen and crying like a baby, past the belief that the universe hates him and is killing off those most important to him, past the awful emptiness of his loss. This is what I loved about my friend when I was alive. He's a skinny little guy who can run like the wind, but at some point he turns and stands his ground. If I weighed more than twenty-one grams I'd grab his hand and lead him up the stairs.

I'm turning into the slide, he thinks over and over and over.

Eddie doesn't know how much time passes, but finally his heartbeats slow and he realizes *nothing bad is happening*. He hasn't seen my face once. His tears dry. He stands, chilly in just his pajama bottoms and bare feet. He works his way slowly back to the steps. I'm gonna be okay, he thinks. I beat it.

And a mouse runs across his foot.

He screams so loud his voice would be hoarse for two days if he were using it and dashes toward the closed door, slipping twice, cracking his forehead on a stair. He kicks the basement door open, then the kitchen door, then the back porch door and is sud denly screaming down the street. Unaware until later of the throbbing in his forehead or the freezing pavement beneath his feet or the wind whistling in the trees around him, he runs. All of Bear Creek is dark; not a streetlight shines, not a car moves. He runs past the station, past the Mercantile and Woody's Grocery, gouging his bare feet in the gravel intersections, feeling nothing. For days afterward, people will talk of the awful shrieking that pierced the black of that night, though no one will know its source.

Exhausted and terrorized, Eddie crawls in under the low branches of a tall pine tree on the courthouse lawn, eight blocks from his house. In the fraction of a second between his feeling of terror and that of safety, I see a window and swoosh through. "*What are you doing here?*"

He glances around, sees nothing.

"*Does the combination of lightning and a tall tree concern you at all?*"

"Who's there?" he says.

I lose him.

"Who's there?"

Another quick window. "*What would be a good next move?*"

When Mrs. Proffit arrives home from church, she finds Eddie sitting in the middle of the living room, soaking wet and out of breath beneath the blazing lights, staring at a blank TV screen.

4

Sorting Out

There were *two* separate voices. One told Eddie to turn into the slide, and the other asked him what he was doing sitting under a tall tree in a thunderstorm. He knows the turn-into-the-slide voice wasn't real. He hears that voice all the time; it's just memory. You hear something that works at one point in your life, and then it comes back at another point in your life when you need it. That's the voice of reason, of common sense.

The *other* one, however, was a *voice*. When he was

running through the streets tearing up his feet, there was not a soul in sight; all of Bear Creek was like a ghost town. And yet there under the tree he *heard* it. His *eardrums* rattled. Now he sits, dried off in his well-lighted room with the voice from under the tree adding to his fears. Have I gone stark raving nuts?

I'd help him, but all his windows are slammed, and painted shut, and nailed.

Eddie hears breathing in his doorway, looks up, and guess who's filling it? Well, not *filling*, because he's only five-six.

"Your mother tells me you're in some distress," Tarter says.

Eddie looks behind Tarter for his mother. She's not there.

"She thought it might be the kind of problem I could be of help with, though it was my idea to come to your room," Tarter says. "I seize opportunities as they present themselves."

Freaked as he is, Eddie's bouncing brain adds this to his list of bad things about not talking: You can't tell your mother to keep her friends out of your room. He looks directly, and inoffensively, at Tarter, displaying no emotion.

"This selective mute thing is not serving you well," Tarter says.

Oh, but it is. Eddie raises his inoffensive eyebrows.

"Do you have any idea what this is doing to your mother?"

Eddie sighs. Technically, that's not talking.

"She blames herself," Tarter says. "She thinks there is something she hasn't done as a parent that is contributing to this. She must endure the loss of her eternal mate and this, too. I think it's time you gave her some respite."

Eddie's look softens, letting Tarter know he heard. But if he were talking, he'd tell him that if his dad was her eternal mate, then she hasn't lost him, has she? He misses his dad as much as his mother does, literally aches when he thinks of him.

"About that distress. Your mother says she found you in quite a state of agitation when she came home this evening. You might have avoided that had you accompanied her to church, but of course that's your choice. At any rate, she believes you're having unsettling dreams, that you're roaming the house at night. She also says she's heard what she calls whimpers of agony out of your sleep."

Eddie does not like his mother telling Reverend Tarter private things about him, and he does *not* like the term "whimpers of agony." He's fourteen, for crying out loud. He gives the reverend more eyebrows.

Tarter sits on the end of his bed. "May I?" It ends in a question mark, but it isn't a question. "I'm aware many of your friends and classmates have already been baptized," he says. "For some reason you haven't taken that step."

That reason would be Eddie's dad, who did not believe that symbolically cleansing your soul by getting dunked in a toga in Arling hot springs has much to do with truly cleansing your soul. Those were Mr. Proffit's words. Also, at one time or another during the year, half the kids in town peed in the hot springs; Eddie knew it for a fact—he used to be one of them—so even if your soul does get cleansed, there's your body to consider. Swimming there is one thing, cleaning up for eternity quite another.

"I believe God is sending you an important message with these terrors," Tarter says.

Terrors? Eddie thinks. A minute ago they were unsettling dreams. But he perks up. What message would God send with *terrors*? As much as he is not a fan of the reverend, if there's a message, he'd like to hear it so he could tell God he *got* it and maybe strike a deal. Eddie doesn't know yet that the universe doesn't deal.

"The Lord works in mysterious ways," Tarter

continues, "and I've pondered your situation extensively. It may very well be the heavenly father is telling you if you turn your life over to him, these fears will subside. A lot has happened to you this year, Eddie. Do you know the story of Job?"

Yeah, Eddie thinks, I know the story of Job. Job is the guy in the Bible who ate it big-time. God brought plague and pestilence down on him. God offed his whole family. When Job didn't complain, God gave him another one and made everything okay. It was a story he used to hear in Sunday school. Eddie got in big trouble when he aired his concerns about that first test family. God threw one whole family away just to see if he could make Job crack? If he were talking, he'd tell the reverend he thought God did a job on Job.

But right this minute, Eddie's thinking, Is he saying God is trying to scare me to test me? Whoa! It seems like that would be a job for the devil.

"It's something to think about," Tarter says.

The reverend doesn't understand that Eddie is not talking because it's one of the few things he can control when everything else is out of control, and it feels *good* not to be sticking his foot in his mouth all the time, like he's done pretty much every day of his life since he can remember. Eddie feels the need for *focus*. . . . I need to understand what's happening to me. I need to understand how the world works, how people can just be there and then not be there, which means I need to keep right on shutting up and watching. And I need to know WHY MY BEST FRIEND BILLY BARTHOLOMEW IS STALKING ME!

"In our church you are required to testify before the congregation prior to your baptism. I have to say that, until you decided to cease all oral communication, you were the most articulate young man your age I've encountered. Along with Billy, of course. I have taken the liberty, with your mother's permission, of going back into your elementary-school files to see some of your previous schoolwork. Though your records reflect to the contrary, I believe you were working three to five years ahead of your grade, when you bothered to finish what you started. I expect that, were you to put your mind to it, you could testify rather handily. Once you do that, and accept the Lord into your life, I guarantee you'll begin to understand."

Eddie takes a deep breath. He likes it when people know how smart he really is. He spent much time in elementary school when that wasn't true. Most people who looked at his records didn't bother to see what he wrote; they just noticed he never finished anything.

Tarter says, "I'll be having dinner here night after tomorrow, thanks to your mother's generosity. I want you to decide by then. I think your life would be much easier. And I think your mother's life would be easier, too. You owe her that."

Mr. Tarter's words irritate Eddie. He's living up to

his reputation; telling you what he wants and just expecting you to do it. But it would be so nice to believe him. If all Eddie had to do was testify and get baptized to get rid of this awful torment, he'd be standing by the side of Arling hot springs with his nose plugs. But to go along with Tarter seems like a betrayal of his father and a betrayal of me. We actually looked forward to Tarter's class as sort of a quest, a proving ground. Tarter was famous among kids for never losing, and we were going to beat him. It wasn't about his religion—we weren't up for messing with God—it was about his harsh discipline. As for his dad, well, Mr. Proffit told Eddie constantly, "Understanding is the key. When something seems mysterious and magical, it's because we don't have enough information." When Eddie would ask if that meant there was no God, Mr. Proffit would say, "Not at all. All that knowledge has to come from somewhere, right, buddy?" It seemed so simple (and it is, but that's because I know what I know). My friend Eddie Proffit, who always asks the best questions, is so tired of being scared, and so isolated without the backing of his father or his best friend, that he is considering giving in just to see if the terror goes away. He could tolerate it if he were only sad. He could tolerate it if he were only scared. But he can't tolerate both.

"One more thing," Tarter says. Eddie's thoughts have been skipping through his mind like a flat rock across a smooth lake. He thought Tarter had left the room. "I know your father had some pretty interesting ideas. They were wrong, but they were interesting. And I know the two of you were close. I truly believe if he had lived, he would have come to understand the truth about God; he was too smart to have missed it. I hope his premature death won't keep you stuck with his old ideas."

Eddie feels a stab in his chest. It seems wrong for Tarter to get a leg up on his father after his father's gone. But what if Tarter is right? What if his dad didn't have all the information about God?

"I'll leave you with your thoughts," Tarter says, and moments later Eddie looks up, and he's gone.

Leaving Eddie alone with his thoughts right now is like leaving him in a loud, crowded haunted house near the end of a Stephen King novel, but he's glad to have one fewer person in it. He is a *mess*. His feet are leaking blood all over his bottom sheet now from the gravel cuts, his time honored strategy of turning into the slide has failed him in a big way, and he *knows* he heard a real voice out there under the tree, just as well as he knows there was nobody out there in the night but him.

He sits in the light of his room with a towel wrapped around his feet and the drapes pulled and chairs propped tight against the closet doors, determined to figure this out. But his brain has a different idea, and before he knows it, he's hopping from Tarter placing a white cloth over his face and laying him back in the hot springs to his father and him gazing through what Mr. Proffit called their "backyard Hubble" at the Milky Way, to actually eating a Milky Way. His head nods a couple of times and his eyes half close and his mind settles on the sledding hill.

That's my cue.

Here's the deal. I can't interfere. It's not like some fancy rule or anything, I just can't, as in couldn't if I wanted to. All I can do is wise him up, help Eddie remember what he already knows, make connections between his world and this one. I can bump him, and I will, because the one thing that is as true out here as it is in the Earthgame is *connection*. Connection is love. Staying connected with Eddie Proffit is as good for me as it is for him, because love is as true on earth as it is in the farthest reaches of the universe.

So I do it.

"Okay if I go down with you?" We're at the top of

Summer's Hill—the sledding hill. It's the first snowfall of the year, and half the Bear Creek population under the age of sixteen crowds the hill with sleds, saucers, old car hoods, and inner tubes.

"I thought you were dead," Eddie says.

"I am. Okay if I go down with you?"

"If you're dead, what are you doing here?"

"I'm going sledding, dummy," I say, "if you'll let me go down with you."

"Didn't you bring your sled?"

"I'm dead. Dead kids don't have sleds."

There are two ways to sled double. Both riders can sit, with the smaller person in front and the back person's feet on the guider, or they can lay on their stomachs, one on top of the other. Given that Summer's Hill dumps onto a road not blocked off for sledders, the second option is safest because you can guide better with your hands than with your feet (though getting run over by a car is of no consequence to me). The top guy pushes to get you going, then jumps on. We have a bit of a problem because dead kids can't guide, but neither can they push, at least not in this Twilight Zone of Eddie's. I'm in his territory, his dream state. I was pushier under the tree because he was in a bit of a crisis situation, but in this case I'm following his lead. So I lay on top of him, and he gets us going, using his hands like ski poles. I don't say anything till we get to the bottom.

"That was fun. Let's do it again."

"You ever see my dad?" he asks.

"No. Want me to look for him?"

He looks at me funny, sensing this is the same voice he heard under the tree, and he pops awake. No more snow, no more sled, no more sledding hill. No more me. The overhead light still burns bright; the chairs are propped tightly under the knobs of both closet doors. The drapes are pulled. The house is quiet as a tomb, and Eddie is sweating so profusely he's about to slip off the bed.

He takes three or four deep breaths and pads quietly from his bed to the door, peers out into the dark hall, takes two quick giant steps to the bathroom and flips on the light. His feet sting like crazy, so he places another towel under them and sits on the toilet. Man, I am going over to the Red Brick Church first thing in the morning to tell Tarter to get the gospel singers ready and skim off Arling hot springs and get me on the fast track to salvation. I have been creeped out one time too many on this day, and I am ending it.

All right then. Done. Decided. He'll go down early in the morning and talk like they're beating the bottoms of his feet with sticks. He reviews the bad trade-offs—he'll be adding three evenings to his All Tarter channel for baptism and confirmation classes, and he'll have to talk to him, which means he'll have to get the way he talks under control because Tarter does not have tolerance for high-speed randomness. He scoffs at the betrayal of me, because he considers

I'm betraying him by trying to scare him into the next decade. No matter. If he doesn't get the craziness out of his life soon, like tomorrow, he'll be strumming his lips with his fingers in Orofino, at State Hospital North. One problem: Within his silence he has found his *only* safety.

5

Black Like Cain

Since his dad and I checked out, Eddie has added considerable mileage to his running and biking routines. A pounding heart has become the different drumbeat to which he marches. (Death brings out the lyricist in me. I know words I never *heard*. In every language.) For one thing, in his mind my evil twin has a harder time keeping up with him if he's on the move, and he can think better, which is about all he's doing these days. Since he's not talking, he's not a lot of fun to hang around with, and he was never all that sociable anyway, so it's not like kids are lining up to be his good buddy. He tends to shoot from the lip with them as much as with adults. Apart from his dad and my dad, I was about the only person who understood him.

I could bump him on these runs because he leaves all kinds of avenues open, but I'm not ready to take the chance of running him off the road. He's wondering today why he's so mad at me. It's not the haunting, he thinks. That's not even real. It couldn't be. But I'm *mad.* I'm mad all the time. Billy gets killed, and then I'm mad at him. That's harsh. But if he were here, I'd punch him. I would. I'd punch him. I mean, how dumb was it to kick a stack of Sheetrock that weighs twice as much as you do and then turn your back on it? Why couldn't you of just paid attention, Billy? Nothin's ever gonna be the same. Nothin'. He quickens his pace.

Once you're dead you know everything turns out okay—in the *way* long run—and I'd like to tell him that, but it's not my place. And the anger has a purpose; to keep the sadness at bay.

His mind bounces to Tarter. Man, I am headed for SO much trouble. No single kid ever took him on and lived to tell about it. That's why I need Billy. If he was here I wouldn't be wimping out getting baptized, 'cause he wouldn't be FREAKING ME OUT ALL OVER THE PLACE. I mean, what if it doesn't even work? What if I go givin' my life to Jesus and Jesus knows I'm just doing it to not be scared? If there's a Jesus, he probably doesn't fall for stuff. I hate it that God and him can get inside your head. Like how are you s'posed to get any privacy?

He runs harder and lets his mind run blank, but Tarter reappears. If he were thinking straight, he'd be way more afraid of Tarter than my silly apparition. I won't talk yet, Eddie thinks. I'll make him give me more time to think.

The incident that cranked up Eddie and me happened in sixth grade, when we heard Tarter made

Albert Redmond stand in front of the class with his arms extended for chewing gum (second offense) and every time Albert complained, Tarter put a book in his hand and then taunted him about not being strong enough to accept the consequences of his actions. When Albert called Tarter a name that rhymes with Albert's father's job driving eighteen-wheelers over the nation's highways, Tarter got him suspended for three weeks and wouldn't let him back until he apologized in front of the entire class for exposing them to "the language of the ignorant and obscene."

Albert's parents lodged a complaint, but Tarter pulled out his ace in the hole, which was really two aces in the hole, which was really two aces on the school board, which was really two aces on the school board who were also aces on the Red Brick Church board. These days he has three aces. Albert went ahead with the apology, but each time he finished, Tarter told him it wasn't "sincere" enough, and after the third time Albert came unglued and screamed the same name he'd called Tarter before, over and over and over again until it became clear to all that Albert Redmond wasn't mentally stable enough to stay in school. Albert works at the sawmill now.

My father told me the day of Albert's expulsion to steer clear of Tarter when I got to high school, but Eddie and I decided we'd make it our mission to get even for all the Albert Redmonds, past and future. We didn't know him very well, but you had to feel bad for Albert because he was one of those guys who can almost completely disappear right in front of your eyes.

We planned to hit Tarter where it hurt. We would keep ourselves out of the kind of trouble Eddie was famous for—shouting out answers and asking questions that had no answers—and challenge Tarter any time he stepped on our rights. I even went so far as to dust off the dog collar to put around Eddie's leg.

Eddie was the one we knew Tarter would go after, because he already had a history from Sunday school.

We were champions of the underdog, Eddie and I, and now Eddie has to go it alone. Only he's enrolled in baptism classes, waving his white flag. But he's not seeing my twisted face and body as much, and he's been sleeping better, so the trade-off seems worth it. I'm staying out of his Twilight Zone until I can find a way to not add to the trauma. Under any circumstances, he's got to figure this one out alone.

So today Eddie runs and he thinks and he runs and he thinks and then he gets his bike and rides and thinks and rides and thinks until he looks at his watch and realizes he is about to be late for his first baptism class, which could add brute strength to his shoulders because you have to hold your arms out one minute for every minute you're late. All of a sudden he remembers nothing of what he thought when he was running and riding and just pedals like a wild man. He arrives at the Red Brick Church gasping for air, with forty-five seconds to spare.

The reverend starts the session introducing Eddie and mildly embarrassing him, asking if he's going to "grace them with words." He reminds Eddie that before he can actually be baptized he must testify and that will require use of his vocal chords. Eddie smiles and the class is off and running.

Then Tarter throws him a curve ball Eddie totally can't hit. He backtracks to Genesis, to the story of Adam and Eve's kids, Cain and Abel. It's one of those mom-and-dad-liked-you-best stories, which ends with Cain killing Abel out of jealousy. Supposedly God put a mark on Cain because of it.

So what? Eddie thinks. Bible says there were only four people on earth, whittled down to three because Abel got whacked. Adam and Eve knew who did it (not exactly *Law & Order* detective work), and unless I don't know my history, mirrors weren't invented yet. So what's the point of a mark?

Everyone who could see it already knew.

Sean Evans, one of the other, younger kids in the class, wants to know what the mark looked like. "Like was it a mole, or a birthmark? A tattoo?"

"No," Tarter says, "none of those things. It's a more significant mark than that."

"Like a mask?" Sean asks.

"Sean, this is a mark that must last through the ages. You want to remember that everyone who could see the mark on Cain already knew what Cain did. What would be the point of that?"

That answers Eddie's original question, but this is beginning to sound like one of those points his dad and Tarter might have hotly discussed on the island of the service station while John Proffit gassed up Tarter's car.

Sean says, "So what was it?"

"It's dark skin," Tarter says. "African Americans wear the mark of Cain."

WHOA! Only there is no whoa! because Eddie's

brain does a giddyap. Instantly he knows he is going to be terrorized by my smiling, decaying mug for the rest of his life because Tarter has crossed a line. Bear Creek is—well, there's no political correctness out here in the universe, so—full of white folks. Eddie knows very few people who aren't. But he is a smart kid, moved by both history and literature. Just because he doesn't stay on one subject very long doesn't mean he doesn't learn it. His favorite book in seventh grade was *The Watsons Go to Birmingham—1963.* It's a funny, tragic, magical book based on a real-life church bombing in Birmingham, Alabama, in 1963 in which four little black girls were killed. The bombing was in response to a huge civil rights movement that rocked the entire country at the time. Eddie was so moved by the story, when he discovered it was true, that he researched the entire civil rights movement, and had he had the attention span to actually write about it, he would have become an instant intellectual celebrity in our school. What he walked away from his research believing was that if you convince yourself someone is less than you, you can treat them any way you want. You can even kill their children. He wished he could be in a room sometime when Tarter informed Michael Jordan about ol' Cain.

Eddie gets up.

Tarter says, "Eddie?"

Eddie looks right in his eyes, smiles sadly, and walks out of the room.

As he walks down the road toward home, Eddie Proffit tells himself he's just going to have to figure out some other way to deal with his terror, because if the Red Brickers got *that* wrong, no way could he trust their God to bail him out of his current hell. He's furious at Tarter, but even madder at me, because if I would just quit *haunting* him all the time, he wouldn't be in this spot. At the same time, because this is the way his mind works, he's thanking me, because he would never have heard Tarter say it if he hadn't gone to those classes, and he might have been sucked in. His mind bounces all over that Bible story.

No wonder my dad fought with Tarter. If Tarter's God made Cain black because he committed fratricide—and Eddie is plenty smart enough to know that word—He must have meant the mark to embarrass anybody who wore it all down through eternity, which goes to at least now. Like, "Here's the deal, Cain, since you offed your brother and I can't put you in jail because we don't have those, everyone down your line of the family is going to have to eat dooky because of what you did. Perfectly good and innocent people will live their lives with this mark, which if you have it, by the way, you will look way better than people without it. I mean, face it, white people are pasty. And if Tarter was right and there are still black people, which there obviously are, then it means God is still mad at them for a crime some guy who lived, like, seven thousand years ago committed. And Cain only murdered his brother. There was this guy a few years back, Jeffrey Dahmer, who killed a bunch of people and *ate* them. What color mark did *he* deserve, and why didn't he get one? And what about the Green River Killer? That guy killed so many people his kids should be rainbows.

My man Eddie is seriously worked up.

I'll bet that's how white people let themselves have slaves. His mind rants on. I'll bet that's why they wouldn't let black people eat at lunch counters with them or pee in the same public restrooms or swim in the same swimming pools. A clarity moves into his mind. People can make excuses for anything, he thinks. Anything.

In his anger, Eddie almost nearly forgets I'm dead and before he knows it, he's standing in front of my dad's house, wishing he could unload all this on me—the real me, not the zombie—get me into serious strategy sessions to bring the reverend down. Eddie wants an all-out assault. He stands on the porch with tears running down his face because there's no one to talk to, no one to tell. He turns around and walks toward the porch steps.

"Eddie?"

My dad's in the doorway.

"You okay, guy?"

Eddie shakes his head.

"Me either," Dad says. "Why don't you come in? I'll buy you a Coke."

Eddie walks back toward my dad and suddenly caves in. "I miss him so much," he says, sobbing. "I need him to talk to. I quit talking because there's no one to talk to." And then he unloads the events of the evening on my father right there on the porch. "Tarter is a pig," he says through gritted teeth when he's finished.

"Can I assume you've resumed oral communication?" my dad says. He's smiling.

Eddie looks around the porch, suddenly aware he's uttered his first words in months.

"Only to you," he says. "I'm not ready to talk to anyone else. Only to you, okay? Don't tell."

My dad raises his hands in mock surrender. "Wild horses . . ." he says. "You didn't actually tell Tarter you were quitting the classes, right? You didn't speak."

"Naw, I just got up and left."

"Look, I know you and Billy were planning—"

"How did you know that?"

"Billy told me. I went to Bear Creek High School, too, you know. Tarter's first year teaching was my junior year. I hated him and he hated me. He didn't have any power when I applied for the maintenance job, or you sure wouldn't see me pushing brooms through the halls."

"I don't get it how somebody who thinks like that can get away with being a teacher."

"There are good teachers and bad teachers, bud."

"Yeah, well, he's a bad teacher."

"You won't get any argument with me, but you can't say that out loud."

"No kidding."

"I went to his church when I was in high school, you know."

"I thought you said you hated each other."

"I did say that," Dad says, "but I've always loved espionage, read spy novels from junior high on, and the one thing I'm sure of is you always want to know your enemy."

"What are you saying?"

"Pretend you left because you weren't feeling well and go back. Don't talk. Just listen. You might learn something you can use later. You have the whole year with him in front of you. You don't have Billy . . ." and then he gets quiet. "Sorry, Eddie. I get hit sometimes. I can't believe . . ." He looks Eddie in the eye. "Look, buddy, I can't take the place of your dad and you can't take the place of Billy, but I know you're not making such a go of it with your mom, and I miss Billy like crazy. We can't replace them, but we can stand in."

Eddie feels a rush of relief.

"When you come across something that seems to need a dad, run it by me. When I come up with something that needs a son, I'll do the same. I won't boss you around and you don't get all kidlike and rebellious on me, and we might just be able to help each other out."

So my dad and my best friend form a clandestine alliance to help them limp through their lives without people they love.

"You want to stay mute as long as you're in the classes," Dad says. "I know you, Eddie Proffit, and if you're talking at all, you're talking all the time. Tarter would smoke you out in a *minute.* He'll bring up the mark of Cain—or wait till you hear what God did to Abraham and Isaac—and you'll be all over him. You and I can have a time every day—

alone time—and you can talk all you want . . . well, not *all* you want, but enough."

Eddie nods.

"The way Tarter sees the mark of Cain," Dad tells him, "is an old Mormon belief. I don't know if they still believe it, but Tarter started out in their church back in his day; got too conservative even for them. He must have brought that little gem with him when he broke off and started this Red Brick thing. He probably doesn't run into much conflict with it because there are no black people here."

I'm going to catch up with Eddie in his crossover time tonight; not talk, but just be there. I think if I show up enough times in a row and don't push it, he'll figure out it's not quite a dream and he can quit seeing me like Jason or Freddy. See, when I'm bumping him, or if I'm just following closely, I see what he sees, through his eyes. I can do that with anyone, even you. Since us dead guys aren't judgmental and we couldn't embarrass you even if we were, it's okay. Anyway, I'm tired of seeing myself through Eddie's eyes, all crunched by that Sheetrock. Even the mortician had me looking better than that.

6

Winter in the Middle of Summer

"So tell me again why you wanted to get baptized?" I'm standing on the sledding hill again, next to Eddie. He thinks it's a dream because it's winter in the middle of summer and because we start our conversations in the middle, like we've been talking all along. I've been slowly working my way in, just like I said I would, disguising my "voice" so he doesn't hear what he heard under the tree and freak himself awake.

"To make you stop haunting me."

"I'm not haunting you. What's the matter with you? I'm your best friend."

"Oh, yeah? Then who's that staring through my bedroom window in the middle of the night, or rooting around in my closet? And who told me to get out from under the lightning?"

"I didn't tell you, I asked what you thought would happen if you didn't."

"Yeah, but you said it in a voice. Like now, only I wasn't dreaming. And besides, I wouldn't have been out there if you hadn't terrorized me into running into the middle of the street in my bare feet."

I say, "Wasn't me."

"Whaddaya think? I did that by myself? Why would I do that?"

"Why would I *do it?"*

"You tell me."

"We gonna go down this hill?"

"And how come you always meet me here? It's the middle of the summer and all of a sudden

there's snow all over everything and everybody's acting like that's the way it's supposed to be."

"This is where we had some of our best times. I just thought it was a good place. Want me to meet you somewhere else?"

"Naw," he says. "You're right. This is fine. We did have a lot of fun here." I watch a dark sadness sweep over him. "I really miss you, man."

"I'm right here."

"Yeah, but you're not real."

"Don't be so sure. So, about the baptism."

"You know, I'm scared all the time."

"Are you sure you need to be?"

He says, "Are you sure I don't?"

I am but don't say it. "Look, I gotta let you figure things out for yourself mostly, What good is being scared doing you?"

"What are you, out of your mind?

"Yeah, and my body. If it's not doing you any good, why don't you quit it?"

"Believe me, if I could I would."

"If that were true," I say, "you would have quit already."

"Man, you are bugging me. This is a dream, you know. I can run us into traffic and scare you back. It's my dream, so I wake up on impact. Who knows what happens to you?"

"Turn into the slide, buddy. You can get rid of the fear by remembering what you've always known. What you've always known better than any of us."

"Turn into the slide? Turn into the slide? I did *that. If you're really dead, you know that. I don't get it."*

"You think that bizarro face you see all the time is me? You think I'd shoot all around through eternity looking like that? Wouldn't I have to be the dumbest guy in four galaxies? Can you hear it? 'Man, you look bad, how'd you do that?' and I'd say, 'Oh, I kicked a two-hundred-pound stack of Sheetrock over on myself.' There's a good way to get into heavenly Mensa."

"Yeah, but how do I know that when I'm awake? This is a dream."

"If it were you that died," I say, "would you come back and scare me out of my pants?"

"I might, once or twice."

"I always was a better friend than you. Anyway, just think about how we were."

"So why did you ask me about getting baptized?"

"Duh!" I say. "We've been dreading Tarter since fifth grade. Now you're going into his class and into his church and he's coming to your house? Why do you think I asked?"

"Bad, huh? You can predict the future?"

"Does it make sense that I can predict the future if it hasn't happened yet? What would that do to your free will?"

"So why are you warning me about Tarter?"

"If you're in the middle of a train tunnel and you hear a loud whistle and see a single light getting bigger and bigger, you wouldn't have much trouble guessing what's up, right?"

"Got it."

7

Dead Authors Beware

On the first day of school, Eddie gets a lot of room. He's a frosh, so it wouldn't be unusual to see his books knocked out of his hand a time or two, or the drinking fountain turned up in his face as he leans over it, but the jocks and the Goths and everyone between watch him coming through the front entrance and ache a little. Losing your dad and your best friend inside a month buys a little extra consideration. A path opens for him between the front door and the lockers.

There's a curriculum element at Bear Creek High School I was pretty psyched up about before I cashed out. In most high schools, freshmen have almost no choices for electives. Math, social studies, English, PE, and science requirements eat up most of your day. But first period at Bear Creek, you can take *any* class you want, provided you can keep up. Eddie and I were going to take *Really* Modern Literature because we both like stories and because Ms. Ruth Lloyd teaches it. She's the school librarian, so it's her only class, and she puts everything into it.

First day, first period, first RML class. Wish I were here. Ms. Lloyd says, "Good morning, ladies and gentlemen."

Everyone but Eddie answers, and he nods and smiles. "Good morning."

"You have signed up for *Really* Modern Literature, where the only requirement is that you read books by authors who are still alive. Can you imagine that? Did you know there were authors who are still alive?"

Everybody laughs. They do know it, but they also know most of the authors *they've* read in the past few years are goners.

"If you want to read fifteen books by Stephen King, you can read fifteen books by Stephen King, though I wouldn't recommend it because most Stephen King books are *long*." She reads off a long list of authors she likes: Grisham, Rowling, Blume, Hinton, Clancy, O'Brien, Crutcher, Curtis, Vonnegut ("but you better hurry"), Lee ("you better keep hurrying").

It's ironic; now that I'm dead I can read authors that are alive. Of course it takes me a microminimillisecond to read a book, because all I have to do is pop into the head of the author right after she or he wrote it. It's like Ultimate Cliff Notes. Dead kids could get good grades really easy, if we could convince anyone to let us take the test. I'm coming to this class with Eddie every day.

Ms. Lloyd goes on with her one requirement. "You have to read one book in common, and because

I am old and smart and you are young and . . . well, young . . . I will decide which book that will be. With the other books, all you have to do to pass the class with an A is take five minutes out of your busy lives to give me the one line in the book that meant the most to you: made you laugh or cry or angry or just made you wiser, *or* if you hated it, a line that is evidence why. Then you move on. I'm assigning one book, *Warren Peece,* by Crutcher. That one we'll discuss in detail."

Lori Combs raises her hand. "Why did you pick that book? He's like the only author on this list I've never heard of."

Ms. Lloyd smiles. "I picked it because it has a lot of bad language, and I thought that might get some of you who tend to get your book reports from the backs of cereal boxes to actually read a book cover to cover. I've been to Mr. Crutcher's website, and from the sounds of things he was lucky to graduate from high school. Those of you who don't consider yourselves happy readers, take heart. Also, the book covers some issues I think are worth talking about. Of course I'll send a permission slip home. I'd appreciate it if you'd just have your parents sign it and don't say what it is, like you do with your report cards."

Sandra Evans, a junior, raises her hand. "How do we know you won't give us an alternate book that is awful and boring, just to punish us for being offended by a book you like?"

"You *don't* know that," Ms. Lloyd says, "and now that you've said it, it sounds like a wonderful idea. Ms. Evans, there is a good chance you will grow up to be a teacher."

Dan Moeltke raises his hand. Dan is a *way* smart senior and a mover and shaker in the Tarter Brigade, aka Youth for Christ. He's in a neck-and-neck race with Kathy Gould for valedictorian of their class. Dan's valedictory address would be very different from Kathy's. "Do you know this Crutcher guy?" he asks.

Ms. Lloyd smiles. "No, I've never met the author. Why do you ask?"

Dan scopes the room. "There have to be twenty-five or thirty students here. That's twenty-five or thirty books. Chris Crutcher could be getting rich off us. I was wondering if you got a kickback."

Eddie multiplies thirty times four dollars and fifty cents.

"You're a very bright young man, Mr. Moeltke. You should sign up exclusively for business classes. You'll be able to take care of your parents in their old age."

"My parents are fully capable of taking care of themselves," Dan says. "Of course I'm also wondering if this book is fit to read."

"Of course you are, Mr. Moeltke. I'm expecting spirited debate from you."

"You'll get it."

"I guess we'll see if you have what it takes to challenge yourself to stretch, Dan."

I ingest *Warren Peece* in the amount of time between when you flip on the light switch and the light comes on. Divided by infinity. Okay, I'm showing off, but if I'm going to keep up I have to know what's going on. The moment I know the book, I know why the likes of Ms. Lloyd wants to use it, why the likes of Dan Moeltke doesn't, why Eddie Proffit will embrace it, and why as I gaze into the tunnel, the light I see is the oncoming train.

8

Protecting Impressionable Minds

One reason dead people are so smart is that we see from a long way away while at the same time burrowing into any heart or mind we choose. I said before most dead folks don't hang around long after they croak. That's because there are far more interesting things to experience in the universe than the narrow story that is life on any given planet, or the even narrower focus of the stories surrounding the people you knew when you were alive. Eddie is the reason I stay. You might think it would be my father.

My father is crippled with grief at my death. He and I lived alone since my mother left when I was three. She had a different dream to chase. Obviously I know where she is now, but that's not part of Eddie's story, and it's not likely to be part of my father's. She just fell in love with someone else, and Dad couldn't make himself fall out of love, so he turned all his attention to me, and to his job, which may not seem like much but gave him access to kids, who he would have been working with had he gone to college and become a teacher. He's what Eddie's dad was: an underachiever in the eyes of many, but not his own. Eddie's dad had the same "bouncing brain" as Eddie, but my dad could have gone on to school easily, even had a track scholarship to a small college in Washington, but he was *so* in love with my mother, and when she decided to stay in Bear Creek and cut hair and make people's finger- and toenails into miniature artists' canvases, he couldn't make himself leave. When I was alive I wondered if he ever regretted not getting out, especially after she left, but now that I'm dead I know he never regretted it a minute. He loves my mother so much, even to this day, that he wouldn't give up the experience of loving her for a Ph.D. in physics. His connection to her is as strong today as it ever was, even though she doesn't feel it. I don't worry about my dad because I know he signed up to play the Earthgame as an optimistic dreamer and he will teach much, and learn much and feel much pain. I believe he will make contributions to the world he never would have made if he hadn't lost me. It's a curiosity with humans, how so much productivity can come from searing pain. Of course, much stagnation also comes from searing pain. Heck, searing pain is big fuel. I'll see my dad in the wink of an eye anyway. Eternity is a pretty cool place.

But Eddie is the only human I know who has a gut-level knowledge of how life on Earth is connected to life in the universe. And since life in the universe is all about freedom, his instinct will always be to move toward freedom on Earth.

Meanwhile, the Eddie train and the Tarter train are speeding toward each other on the same track, and I am almost giddy to watch the crash.

"Ruth Lloyd has assigned a book to her literature class that should raise all our red flags," the Reverend Tarter says. The weekly church board meeting is winding down and the reverend is bringing up one last piece of what he considers important business. "Dan Moeltke brought it to my attention. You all know Dan; he's president of Youth for Christ. Apparently the book has some pretty rough language, and it tackles issues better left to responsible parents. Dan went to the author's website and came back with some interesting information, most of which is included in this handout I have for you." He passes three stapled sheets to each of the seven board members. "Long story short, the author is relatively obscure, has ten books out, no best-sellers. He presents himself as a child and family therapist, though as near as I can tell he has only a bachelor's degree. He's a self-proclaimed nonreader who spent some time as a teacher in alternative education, I'm assuming because he couldn't cut it in the public schools. Just the influence we need on our kids, huh? The real red flags come up in the areas of homosexuality—he comes down squarely on the side of legalized gay marriage—and drug abuse. The man believes drugs should be decriminalized.

"The book in question, according to Dan, is filled with four-letter words, has a gay character as one of the central figures, taunts fundamental Christianity, and promotes defiance of authority, particularly teachers and parents. My word, a minor character even gets an abortion."

The board members shake their heads in that what's-the-world-coming-to way that most adults recognize. "What's the world coming to?" Florence Gifford, the one female board member, asks. The question is rhetorical. Florence believes she knows what the world is coming to. An end.

Samuel Cromwell, one of three church board members who is also on the school board, speaks up. "This Crutcher sounds like some kind of pervert or something. What *didn't* he put in this book?"

"Nothing I can think of," Tarter says. "Dan says he seems to have grown up in the hippie generation and simply never got over it. One thing that offended Dan was that almost all his books have an athletic backdrop, but Dan found none of the values he's come to cherish through athletics in this book. You all know Dan is a scholarship-quality athlete, so I guess he can claim some expertise there."

"Is this the course my daughter calls *Really* Modern Literature?" Maxwell West asks. "I may have signed a permission slip for that book. Montana said it was just a routine form for all of Ms. Lloyd's classes."

"Well, you might want to take a closer look at what you sign from now on," the reverend says.

Montana West is not exactly the daughter Mr. West

thought he was raising. He gave her a perfect cowgirl's name, but he got a girl with more piercings than she has places for holes and tattoos that would make a Marine green with envy. The brightest color she wears is black.

Todd Griggs sits forward. Todd is a farmer and a lumberjack, has been on both the church board and the school board for almost eight years. He's a decent guy, and a true believer, one who never questions Tarter because he believes the reverend is blessed with divine wisdom. "So what's the plan, boss?" he says.

"Actually," Tarter says back, "I can't very well openly take on a respected colleague on a matter of curriculum choice, and I like Ruth Lloyd as a person, so we need a concerned parent to bring a formal challenge to the use of the book in general. That will assure a board hearing at some point. I think we can sit back and watch for a while, because our Mr. Moeltke has taken the bull by the horns. Youth for Christ is nearly fifty students strong in the high school, and they have formal club status. I think we lodge the complaint and let them take the lead. Our position will be a lot stronger if it's backed by students."

Maxwell West volunteers to take the formal challenge to Mrs. Madison, the principal, tomorrow morning, knowing that will take the book out of the kids' hands until the school board settles the matter. Since he's not a school board member, yet, there is no apparent conflict of interest, and it will also send a message to his daughter not to try to slip anything else past the old man. He will march into the office first thing in the morning. The members of the church board agree that this move will be their first strike in their new battle to clean up the curriculum and return decency to education.

I'll bet that what returns will be war to the West household. I'm *dead*, and I'm afraid of Montana West.

Maxwell West storms into the office the next morning, lending new meaning to the word "indignant," demanding to see the principal, along with Ruth Lloyd. Mrs. Madison and he talk cordially once the door is closed, while an office aide goes to the library to get Ms. Lloyd. Mrs. Madison is the lead soprano in the Red Brick Church choir. Together they also lend new meaning to the term "slam dunk."

I'm hovering above the windowsill in Ms. Lloyd's class, because I can, when she surprises everyone. "I need you to pass your copies of *Warren Peece* to the front of the room," she says as the students settle into their seats.

"How come?" Sherry Green asks. "I'm not finished with it."

"You are for now," Ms. Lloyd says, and there isn't a student in the room who can't see she's ready to lynch someone, "unless you have a copy of your own. If you do, I advise you to carry it, cover facing out, to every class, to lunch. Read it on the lawn before school and during breaks. Just don't open it in class."

Montana West raises her hand, which *has* to be a

first for Montana West. "Was my dad in the office challenging this book? Is that why he was here? Was he? You better tell me, Ms. Lloyd."

"I'm afraid I'm not allowed to divulge that information just yet," Ms. Lloyd says.

"Well then, just don't say anything if it's true. Is my dad trying to get this book banned?"

Ms. Lloyd smiles.

Montana bounces her forehead off her desk. "Does anyone in this room have parents willing to adopt me? I don't eat much; in fact, I'm anorexic, so I don't eat anything. I pay for my own skin punctures and I prefer to live underground in the dark, so an unfinished basement will work just fine. I'll use it to hunker down after I kill my father."

"No need to break the law," Ms. Lloyd says, "though I feel a little like it myself right now." She moves in front of her desk and leans against the edge. "Folks, I've seen this before. They'll tell you it's about family values and Christian values and morality and our need to get control over our educational system. But it's about you. That's it. Just you. If you're going to stop this, you're going to have to stop it yourselves. Decide whether you think your mind is strong enough to hear tough stories, told in their native tongue—and let the censors know. I can holler about this all day long, but I'm the person who brought it into school, so my voice won't mean much." Eddie watches Ms. Lloyd carefully, and she seems pretty upset. If he could see what I see, he'd back up, because she's about one click of temper from exploding right in front of the class.

And my man Eddie is only a couple of clicks behind her. So far the story has captivated him. The characters aren't like him, but they're struggling and they don't even want much. The gay character just wants to be allowed to be what he is, but no one understands. The sixteen-year-old thinking about an abortion is so confused and terrified she doesn't know whether to keep the baby or not, and has no one to turn to. In fact, to the point where Eddie has read, she's hiding the pregnancy, fantasizing about leaving the baby in a Dumpster. She won't, but that's how scared she is. Man, Eddie thought at first, if there's a problem this Crutcher guy doesn't stick into his book, it must be because he doesn't know about it. You couldn't find this many problems in a zoo. But he has fallen into the story because, while he might have thought it excessive before this last summer, finding the dead bodies of two people he loved dearly in the space of a month has changed his perspective on how bad things can get. Suddenly he feels a rush of strength. I've lost all I'm willing to lose, he thinks, and if he'd open up a window or two he'd hear me cheering. My dad would whack me across the back of the head if I let somebody tell me what I can read or what I can think. He sits back in his seat, his mind bouncing from his dad to backyard catches to exploding truck tires. When it comes time to pass his copy of *Warren Peece* forward, he pretends to add his to the stack but discreetly places it back into his backpack.

9

The Universe Takes a Hands-off Position

The word *surprise* in any credible English dictionary might well have a picture of the Reverend Tarter's face on the evening Eddie shows up again for baptism classes. It's subtle, but he can't wipe it off. "Mr. Proffit, I thought we'd lost you."

Eddie flashes a quick smile and a raise of the eyebrows. He wants to be valuable to his cause. If the church is infiltrating the school, then the school should infiltrate the church. My man Eddie Proffit is gonna be a steely-eyed spy dude.

"I guess you came to see all you had to lose," Tarter says.

Eddie nods and looks at the ground.

"Edward," Tarter says, "I want you to get used to the idea of speech. No matter how well you do in these classes, I am not going to allow your baptism if you don't testify. I know there is nothing organically wrong with you, and if there is, in fact, something mentally wrong with you, it's nothing God can't cast out. So you may as well give in and begin talking."

Eddie smiles again, holds Tarter's hard stare.

"Suit yourself," Tarter says. "You know the rules. I won't bend them. I would however, if you'd like to ease back into it, be open to anything you'd like to give me in writing."

Eddie keeps right on smiling.

"Very well. Back to our lessons. Edward, I'm aware you missed the second half of class last time. Am I to assume that you took issue with our explanation of the mark of Cain?"

Eddie shakes his head no.

"That was the point at which you left; was that a coincidence?"

He nods. Eddie won't normally play twenty questions; rather, he looks away to avoid it. But he needs to make the reverend a believer.

"What you didn't stay for was the explanation," Tarter says. "Our belief doesn't make us bigots; the mark of Cain is simply a fact of life. We don't look down on African Americans, and we know those who live good lives will also go to their reward."

Yeah, Eddie thinks, but I'll bet it's not the same as our reward. And I'll bet their heaven isn't in the same place as our heaven. And if the only people who get into ANY heaven are those who follow the *true* word of God, and the Red Brickers have it, then how many black people are going to believe the "truth"? You'd have to be out of your mind to believe a truth that makes second place the best prize you can win.

At twenty-one grams, there's no room for color, nor a need, but the essences of Martin Luther King, Jr., and Malcolm X and Joe Louis are all out here, and they have full universal privileges. Jack the Ripper is here also, and Lizzie Borden, so even though Tarter isn't correct, he has nothing to worry about.

"Well, I guess we've said all that needs to be said about the mark of Cain. It doesn't apply to any of us anyway, right?"

Eddie looks around the room. Why doesn't anyone else question him? he wonders. There are seven other kids in this baptism class. Youth for Christ has to number close to seventy junior high and high school kids. They must've all heard the same garbage I just heard about the mark of Cain. Did not one of them question it? Or walk out?

What Eddie doesn't know is that's more a tribute to Tarter's powerful presence than to the YFC's bigotry. Most of them will mature and realize the foolishness of such a notion, and frankly, it doesn't affect them directly in the moment. Such is the nature of many humans. It is not the nature of Eddie Proffit.

The rest of the lessons go down easily, mostly because Eddie doesn't take them seriously. He doesn't openly question their veracity, only makes sure he remembers the "facts" for his written work. At the end of the session, which includes obligations toward the church in terms of tithing and work hours, Tarter says, "Edward, I'd like you to stay a few minutes after class tonight, if that's possible."

When the others are gone, Tarter motions for Eddie to take a seat, which he does. "Edward, I want to push your testimony and baptism forward, if we can. I think, because of all you've been through, that you can be a major force in a project we're taking on at the high school. I'd like you to be a full member of Youth for Christ within the next two weeks. To make that happen, I'll need to tutor you and you'll need to start talking again."

Eddie looks directly at Tarter. His expression says he'll consider it. My man is getting *so* good at lying through his eyes. Tarter is unaware that Eddie is ahead of him on the *Warren Peece* issue, and even though Eddie's name and "trouble" usually appear back-to-back in Tarter's brain, he believes Eddie's fear is still driving him. Even in death, I'm an unknown quantity.

"Very well then," Tarter says. "You'll know more when you need to. I've asked a couple of members of Youth for Christ to contact you. I'll be doing more work with your mother, and I'll coordinate that with your accelerated mentoring." His expression softens. "I know things have been tough for you, Eddie. We'll get through all this. I won't abandon you."

I catch up with Eddie on an after-school run. Mr. Pederson, the cross-country coach, hands out workout sheets and mileage charts on the first day of practice and lets the runners choose routes from those posted. Each runner has the choice of three or four different routes per day. Eddie runs alone two days a week, and with the majority of his teammates on others. Today is a solitary run. On these days, depending on how he's feeling, he may run a given course two or three times. The farther he goes, the deeper he gets into himself and the calmer he feels. He will definitely be one of the three top runners as a freshman. The two of us would have been hard to beat.

"Hey," he says to me before I make any spiritual noise.

"Hey," I say back.

"Is this really you?"

"What does it matter?"

"That's right," he says. "I remember you from my dream. You think you're Alex Trebek. All your answers come in the form of questions. You can be as annoying dead as you were alive.

"Your dad was right," he says. "It was smart to stay in Tarter's baptism class. Bet you anything I'm gonna get an earful of this book thing when he comes over tonight. It has to be him behind this. Maxwell West is a big-time guy in the church. No way he does anything without Tarter knowing. He passes the collection plate and hands out the grape juice and that funny bread for Communion. This is Tarter's skullduggery for sure. I like that word. Skullduggery."

As Eddie starts into a long hill, he picks up his pace. I could never figure out how he did that when we ran together. Eddie kills guys on hills. It's easy for me now, though. I just float. *"Montana's the cool one. She's* so *hacked off. I'd love to be at their house when this all gets out in the open. There's gonna be parent-child conflict."*

No argument there.

"Bet she's giving her dad a load right this minute," he says. "She's not exactly a chip off the old block."

His mind jumps to his own dad. "Man, my dad would crap his drawers over all this," he says, and his pace increases even more. Eddie Proffit is eating this hill up. "He would put the school board on notice. *Speaking of crap, you know what's really crap? Of course you do, you're dead. I'll tell you anyway."*

He's right, I do know, but I let him tell me.

"What's really crap is that book was making me feel less lonely and they want to take it away. Now that I have you, and your dad, I feel better anyway, but think of all the people who don't have you or your dad. The guys who want this book out of here thinks it's a sin if somebody thinks a 'bad' word, or considers a 'bad' idea. They don't care if the characters seem like friends to people who don't have any. I bet God's not really like that. And I'll bet it ticks Him off big-time when he sees them using him to get their way. I wouldn't be surprised if we have a hurricane."

He's right and he's wrong. The universe isn't like that. But it doesn't tick the universe off one bit. The universe is loving enough to let what happens happen. The universe has no interest in the outcome.

When Eddie starts into the second circuit of his workout today, he looks over and sees Chad Nash. Chad's so invisible at Youth for Christ he resembles me. He's at church every Sunday and he hangs around the edges of the after-school meetings, but you don't hear a word from him. He says, "Hey, Eddie."

Eddie looks over.

"Okay if I run with you?" Chad says.

Eddie nods.

Eddie seems easy to talk to, and since *he's* not talking, he's no danger as a rat. I know from one look, that's what Chad's looking for. Course Chad doesn't know that when he runs with Eddie, he runs with me, who is also no danger as a rat.

Chad's dad was a NCAA decathlon champion fifteen years ago. He's a big, buff, outgoing guy with

Red Brick Christian family values that don't sweep wide enough to include his son, though his dad doesn't know that. I didn't know it until just this second. Chad Nash is gay, which has him scared spitless because of his membership in YFC. It's like if you were in the KKK and discovered your biological father is Jewish. I'm catching up on Chad's history while we run, which includes terror at disappointing a father who is loud and clear in his devotion to Leviticus, the go-to Old Testament guy for Christians who think gayness and badness are the same thing.

Chad knows Eddie is on the fast track toward baptism and membership in Youth for Christ, but Eddie seems different. He's praying Eddie will be an ally because he is *way* tired of hiding out.

"My parents won't let me have friends outside the church," Chad says, "and I hear you're gettin' baptized."

Eddie slows his pace to match Chad.

"YFC is coming out strong against *Warren Peece*. I can't tell if you like the book or not, but I do and

I'm going to have a tough time going along." He runs in silence a minute or so, breathing way harder than their pace requires. I *feel* it. He wants to just say it. His secret has been exploding inside him. Truth is, Eddie already knows, or assumes, and couldn't care less. Mr. Proffit raised Eddie to worship math and science. Random chance assigns somewhere between eight and twelve percent of the population gay, about the same as left-handers.

Eddie looks over at Chad to let him know he hears.

"*Warren Peece* is the first book I've ever read with . . . with characters who seem like they could be my friends," he says. "That Mitch guy, he's so cool, like, one of the coolest characters in the book." Mitch is a gay character in the story who, after many attempts, finally stands up loud and strong, like Chad wishes he could. "I just kept going back and reading the parts about him. When Ms. Lloyd told us to pass the book in, I almost couldn't breathe. It felt like I lost a friend I can't get back. Hey, could we slow down a little?"

Eddie slows more, smiles, trying to tell Chad without words that everything's cool, but Chad is way too wrapped up in getting it all out to read him. "Man, my family." He stops. "I'm gay, Eddie."

Eddie stops with him, shrugs.

"My dad's a decathlon champion, my brother's got a scholarship to play football at Michigan, and I'm a frigging homo."

Eddie lays his hand on Chad's shoulder.

"Anyway," Chad says, "I know they want you to start talking again, but don't tell anybody, okay? I mean, I know you're getting baptized and joining YFC and everything, but you always seemed like somebody a guy can tell stuff. I always wanted to be friends with you and Billy, but you guys were always off on your own. Don't tell anybody, okay? Please?"

Eddie zips his lips.

"Thanks, man," Chad says. "I was so scared to say

anything, except I was more scared not to, like I was going to blow up. We're supposed to come out all together for getting rid of that book, YFC, I mean, only I can't. I just can't. It would be like turning my back on a friend or something."

Eddie nods.

I whip over into Chad and experience the massive relief. They start jogging, slow. "I'm scared all the time," Chad says after a couple hundred yards cooling down. "I'm scared people will find out, scared they already know. I'm scared somebody might do something like they did with that kid in Laramie, Wyoming."

Eddie makes a fist and shakes his head no. Eddie Proffit doesn't weigh 125 pounds. The only kid in our class he could whip with his fists checked out under a hail of Sheetrock. But if you saw him make the fist, you'd believe no harm will come to Chad Nash on Eddie Proffit's watch.

10

Holy War Wholly Declared

"Dang, it feels good to *talk*," Eddie says. He and my dad are having lunch in the janitor's room with me, only I'm not eating and they don't know I'm here, and Eddie is catching up full speed.

"This is the place to do it," Dad says, nodding toward the door. "Door's three inches thick and locked. The band could be playing the "1812" Overture in here and not a soul could hear it. What did you bring me?"

Eddie reaches into his lunch sack and brings out two

extra turkey sandwiches and a thermos of clam chowder.

"This is such a great trade-off. All I have to do is let you talk and I get lunch."

"And you don't even have to listen," Eddie says.

"True, but I do, because I am an educator who believes in showing respect to my customers, unlike some I know."

Eddie chuckles.

My dad says, "Oh, I don't get to call myself an educator?"

"Well, you're the . . . yeah, I guess."

"Yeah, I guess," Dad says. "I may come face-to-face with more students in a day than any teacher in this building. And I almost always deliver."

"And you're pretty smart," Eddie says.

"And I'm *way* smart, as you guys like to say," Dad says back.

"What do you think about Mr. West challenging *Warren Peece*?"

Dad says, "Tell me this doesn't have the reverend's fingerprints all over it."

"I'm glad you said that," Eddie says. "He put me on the fast track to salvation, so I have a feeling he has plans for me."

"Fast track?"

Eddie explains how, for the next few weeks, his life will have about three hours a day without Tarter in it. It's an exaggeration, but not by much.

"Hooo," Dad says. "You must have ticked someone off in another life."

"No lie . . . you were right, though," Eddie says. "It was smart for me to stay in those classes because I'm, like, the perfect spy. I don't even have to lie 'cause I don't talk. I mean, they got the book pulled for now, but they haven't won yet. It goes through at least one hearing, maybe two. A whole bunch of kids in that class were really liking it; it's got all kinds of bad language and stuff. But that's not the only reason they like it."

"Doesn't hurt, though, does it?" Dad says.

"Nope."

"Eddie, you better get used to the idea of that book being gone. The in-school meeting is a formality. The principal of this school is a hard-line Red Bricker. If she deems the book unworthy, it's done. And the school board is loaded with more Red Brickers. You've got three members who are active members of Tarter's congregation."

They're both quiet a minute, which is like a record for Eddie when his "mute" button's off. Then my dad says, "Eddie, when you start talking again for real, don't you think you should look at making some new friends?"

"I've got friends."

"You've got people you know. But you and Billy were together almost all the time. You ran together, you biked, you hung out. You got turned down by girls. You're going to need to fill up some time."

"I didn't need Billy to get turned down by girls. I was good at that all by myself." Eddie wants to tell him about me, that he's nearly convinced I'm not all the way gone, that we're talking, and that once he let the possibility exist that it might really be *me*, all the really scary stuff in his life went away. He thinks that might help my dad, too. After our run yesterday, Eddie slept like a baby. But he doesn't know how Dad would react. I could tell him: he would think someone had loosened all Eddie's screws. Another reason I don't bump my dad is, there is *no* way. If he *had* any windows and I went in, he'd be running down the street in his bare feet, just like Eddie, only he'd never regain his sanity.

"Yeah," Eddie says, "I should probably find some friends, but there's just nobody like Billy. I mean he was a goof and everything, but he sure was a guy you could talk to. I wish he was here now to do some plotting with me. He didn't like to get in trouble, but he didn't mind if I did."

Dad says, "I suppose the two of you would have gotten yourselves into so much trouble the school janitor would have had to bail you out." Dad shakes his head. "When I went to school, it was all you could do to get most of us to read a book. They don't want to be banning one most of the kids like. Most of them do, right?"

"Yeah," Eddie says. "It's a cool book. When Ms. Lloyd told us to pass them in today, I pretended the one that was passed to me was mine and just stuck mine back in my backpack. I'm gonna finish it."

Dad reaches into his desk drawer and pulls out a copy of his own. "Thought I ought to take a look at it myself," he says. "I figure anything Tarter doesn't want you guys reading must be pretty good liter-chur." He says it like that. Literchur. He turns the book over in his hands. "Tell you what, Eddie Proffit, if this book is going to get read in your class, you better get some kids together. Ms. Lloyd doesn't have a chance by herself. Tarter's got the principal and three school board members in his pocket. It's going to take a pack of teachers and a whole bunch of kids to keep this baby on the shelf. In my day it was *Slaughterhouse Five*. That book doesn't even have a bad guy. A book about nothing but being decent, and Tarter got it removed. And back then the school board and the church board had no overlap. He couldn't have been more than five years older than us that first year teaching. We thought he was gonna be cool. But he got rid of that book with his charming personality alone."

"I'd want to read it even if it's a rotten book, now that he doesn't want me to," Eddie says. "Man, I wish Billy were here."

Dad says, "Well, remember one thing, Eddie. You have rights. Just because you're not twenty-one doesn't mean you're not an American. You just need to know what rights you have and how to access them. And as far as Billy is concerned, remember this: We keep those we love alive with the acts we commit in their names."

Eddie and I are intercepted by Dan Moeltke as he walks through the front entrance the next morning, although you don't really intercept *me* unless I want to be intercepted. Dan puts his big ol' quarterback's hand in the middle of Eddie's back and leads him to an empty classroom. Within a few minutes nine other upperclassfolks join them. Eddie recognizes them as student officers of YFC.

"Hey, Eddie," Monica Bechtel says.

"Hey, Eddies" bounce around the room.

Eddie nods.

Dan gets to it. "Did Reverend Tarter talk with you last night? He said he would."

Did he ever, Eddie thinks, and nods. I thought I'd never get to bed. According to Tarter, this Crutcher is promoting a *lot* of evil. He's got gay characters, he's got blasphemers, he's got Lord's-name-in-vainers. Tarter stayed past midnight giving Eddie the lowdown on what he expected from him at the school hearing once he got baptized.

"Good. Look, we know you've had a really tough year, especially this last summer."

Eddie's expression doesn't change.

"And none of us can tell you how happy we are that you've decided to take Jesus as your personal savior."

Eddie grimaces in the affirmative. It's easy to see he's nervous. Dan Moeltke is a big deal, in YFC and in the school. He's a two-sport athlete with a near-perfect grade point average, and unless you were raised by wolves, you pretty much have to think he's cool.

"We know you're almost ready to testify at church," Dan says. "Baptism comes right after that, and Reverend Tarter says you'll be talking soon."

Eddie nods.

"You'll be a full-fledged church member then, which makes you automatically a member of YFC. We're thinking of making you an honorary officer. At school, we're a service group. You know about the food drives we've sponsored and the group trip to Mexico to build houses for unfortunates. Those things will all be available to you." Dan pauses, lowers his voice. "We're also going to spearhead a student-led drive to bring decency back into the school curriculum."

Eddie smiles, opens his eyes as if hungry to join. He's hot to be a spy guy.

"I'm glad you see the need," Dan says.

Here comes the book-banning strategy.

"Everybody discounts teenagers," Dan says. "Adults believe we don't think for ourselves, that we're morally immature. This group—" and he sweeps his hand to indicate those around him—"knows this is the perfect time to prove them wrong. We all know the best way to keep your mind pure is to keep evil thoughts out. *Warren Peece* is evil, plain and simple. The language is disrespectful and obscene; the Christians in the book are portrayed as mean-spirited and controlling. There's a gay character at the center of everything. The book, in its entirety, is simply a lie. We're going to come out swinging against it."

It's hard for Eddie to keep a neutral face. He loves the book, and he loves it more as he hears Tarter's words come out of Dan Moeltke's mouth. It's hard not to like Dan, and if you're in with these guys you'll never hurt for people to hang out with, but Eddie kind of likes the champion-of-the-underdog role, too, especially when the underdog is him. He nods. I'm lyin' scum, he thinks, but I'm righteous lyin' scum.

"We think you can be a big factor in the outcome of this challenge," Dan says, and the others agree. "Because you've been through all you have, people will listen to you. When you start talking, we want you to think about what you'll say. I could see you holding my position in YFC before you're out of high school. If you're an honorary officer this year, that will give you a two-year head start on most."

"I'll be the head after Dan graduates," Monica purrs. "I'm looking forward to working very closely with you." I feel my man Eddie begin to weaken, so I give him a bump. He doesn't feel a thing. Monica touches Eddie's forearm, and even *I* feel his goose bumps.

The first period bell rings, and they break to head for class. Dan puts a hand on Eddie's shoulder. "We're counting on you, man."

11

GOOD GUYS AND BAD GUYS

"Okay, dead man, you owe me big," Eddie says to me as he rounds the corner on the dirt road and starts the climb toward the abandoned radar site on Burgess Peak. Burgess rises above town like a majestic mini-Matterhorn, its peak jutting into the thin air like a spire. Ooooo. I'm waxin' poetic, which is another thing you can do when you're dead. If Eddie knew how easy these runs are for me now, I'd get an earful. If I had an ear.

I say, "How do you figure I owe you?"

"Bailed out when I needed you most," he says. "Left me running by myself, mostly, and now nobody's covering my back. But you can make up for some of it by helping me spy. And you can prove yourself. See, most of the time I still think you're really just a Fig Newton inside my demented head, as in not real. But if you could, like, tell me some stuff I couldn't know . . . well, you could prove yourself."

"You're asking a dead guy to prove himself?" I say back. "Man, you got some huevos. What if I'm connected big-time out here? You might want to be nicer to me. Making me prove myself, well . . ."

"See, that's all stuff I'd expect you to say, which is why I think it's me."

So I say, "How 'bout that Sputnik?" in Russian, and you should see that little bugger pick up his pace.

A mustachioed man in his late fifties smiles at the YFC council from a PowerPoint display projected onto a screen pulled down from the ceiling in a small auditorium off the foyer in the Red Brick Church. Eddie is invited to the meeting and was late because he ran farther than he meant to, because he knows *he* couldn't have made up that Russian. Dan Moeltke was late also, so everybody's just settling in. Dan stayed to work out some new plays with Mr. Casteel, the football coach. No YFC meeting starts without Dan Moeltke.

I, on the other hand, was not late, because dead kids are never late.

"If we orchestrate this correctly, we can make a big impact on the community and on our school," Dan says as Eddie finds his seat. "I put this display together from images on Crutcher's website. This guy is trouble, but I think not all that bright. He brags about having read only one novel the whole time he was in high school, and Cathy found a way to get his college transcripts from Eastern Washington. The guy operated at C level."

Everybody chuckles at the pun.

"A lot of people think he's a Ph.D. in psychology or something, probably because he talks a lot about his life as a child and family therapist, but I couldn't find anything that indicated he even went to graduate school. He's pretty old, so it's possible you could get into that business without much education back when dinosaurs roamed the earth."

Dan moves through the website, while the kids fill paper plates with cookies shaped like crucifixes, compliments of Rachel Horn's mom. Dan skips quickly through highlights of Crutcher's work, including middle and high schools he's visited in the past year along with boring photographs taken during those visits. Even if you're dead, they're boring. How many pictures can you look at of a guy with an arm draped over some kid's shoulder or signing a book? Dan clicks on a section titled CC SOUNDS OFF and reads excerpts of Crutcher's explanation of his use of offensive language, pointing out that he makes excuses for school shooters and promotes other books of questionable taste, like *To Kill a Mockingbird* (which was that one book he read in high school) and *The Things They Carried*, a highly offensive book by a Vietnam vet, Tim O'Brien. "And look at this," Dan says, bringing up the cover to *The Lovely Bones* by Alice Sebold. "The narrator of *this* book is *dead.* How offensive is *that*? Claims to know what heaven is all about." He clicks another section, in which Crutcher gives tips to educators who are faced with censorship challenges. Dan laughs. "This guy *knows* he is going to be censored," he says. "He *knows* his writing is offensive, to the extent that he even arms teachers who want to promote his indecency with ammunition when his books are found out. He even has a ten-point plan to battle censorship."

The natives are getting restless, so Dan kills the PowerPoint. "This guy makes somewhere between twenty-five and forty school visits a year," he says. "He goes to schools in every state, spreading his evil drivel. If you were to read his other books, you'd get intravenous drug use, sex outside marriage, masturbation; I could go on and on." He walks over to the cookies and paper cups of punch. "But I won't. We've seen enough. We know what we need to do. The building meeting was held today and Reverend Tarter says it now goes to the school board." He bites off the base of a chocolate-chip crucifix. "Look, guys, far more teachers came out *against* cleaning up the curriculum than not, so we need to make a big splash at the board meeting." He looks to the back of the room, where Eddie sits in his sweats. "Eddie, my man, we're counting on you."

Eddie stuffs two cookies into his mouth and raises a fist.

"I've gone through *Warren Peece* with a fine-tooth comb." Dan passes out several sheets of paper. "The first sheet lists all the offensive words and phrases in the book and catalogs them according to page number. I didn't want to ask the rest of you to read through all this garbage, so it's all right there. This second page is a list of what we YFC members consider offensive issues. Those will be our speaking points when we face the school board."

There has to be at least one person in here who knows this is bogus, Eddie thinks. In fact there are, but if you're going to take on Dan Moeltke, you better do your homework and bring your lunch, because he's as good on the debate team as he is on the football field, and he can humiliate you either place.

When I was alive I liked to read stories with good guys and bad guys, and in fact I thought if there weren't good guys and bad guys, it wasn't really a story. What I'm watching here *is* a story, and a pretty darn good one, but I'm bopping around in and out of everybody's head and heart, and I can't find any real bad guys. Moeltke believes he's doing what he's doing for a greater good and that it connects him, and anyone who agrees with him, with God. The Reverend Tarter is passionate in his belief that if Christian adults don't step up and protect kids, they aren't fulfilling their responsibility to God or to mankind and that the world literally is going to hell in a handbasket. Eddie's mother just wants God to love her and take away the pain. Ms. Lloyd believes as passionately in the healing power of stories as Reverend Tarter does in the healing power of God. *Those are all good guys. They want good things.* The principle characters here are mad at one another for what they *believe*, so maybe the fact that they look good or bad to *one another* can take the place of good and evil in this story, should I actually try to get it down on paper, which I've been thinking would be a good idea.

I mean, wouldn't it be cool if I could figure out how to turn this conflict into a book that humans could read and talk about? It could be what I leave, and what Eddie stays with. Think of it—a book with no good guys or bad guys, like it is out here in the universe. Want me to throw you a real curve? Well, here it comes, whether you want it or not, 'cause dead guys do what they want. Judas—or at least the twenty-one grams that *was* Judas—is out here. You know, the guy who ratted out Jesus? I mean, if you want to know about bad guys, who better to talk to, right? Know what he said? He said it was such a relief to be dead because teaching people the extremes of betrayal required him to be greedier and more devious than most souls could tolerate for long. Anyway, it wouldn't be a bad thing to have a book with my friend Eddie Proffit as a main character, but first I have to see how the climax goes.

12

Jesus Loves a Good Book

Ms. Madison strides from her principal's office to the library, pushes the doors open like a sheriff entering a saloon, and crosses to the main desk, where she stands, impatient. When you see her come for a kid this way, you pray for him. Ruth Lloyd finishes checking out a book to Rick Sellers and points Abby Clark to the nonfiction section for a book on the caveman *Australopithecus boisei*. Man, I swoosh into a room and instantly know *every*thing. Too bad I don't have earthly needs; I could make a killing on *Jeopardy*.

Mrs. Madison says, "Could I speak with you in the back room, Ruth?"

"Of course."

The door is barely closed when Mrs. Madison says, "Ruth, do you value your job?"

"Of course," Ms. Lloyd says back, and she's on guard. "Why would you ask a question like that?"

"A number of the kids in your literature class have finished *Warren Peece*. You were ordered to collect and keep those books until after the results of the challenge."

"Which I did."

"Could I see them?"

"Mrs. Madison, are you accusing me of something?"

"Not yet," Mrs. Madison says. "But in my outer office this afternoon, I heard four students discussing the ending to that book. You specifically said you were less than three-quarters through it."

"That wouldn't stop some people from reading ahead," Ruth says.

"One student said she finished it last night."

"It's restricted in school," Ms. Lloyd says, "not in bookstores or libraries or the internet, or anyplace else with a shred of common sense remaining." She retrieves the box of confiscated books.

Mrs. Madison takes a quick count. "How many students in the class?"

"Twenty seven."

"There are only twenty-six books here."

"Eddie Proffit indicated he'd left his at home."

"Eddie Proffit doesn't talk."

"I said *indicated*, Mrs. Madison. When I counted only twenty-six books, he opened his backpack to show me it wasn't there. I told him to bring it the next day."

"And he hasn't?"

"Not yet. Mrs. Madison, do you really think Eddie, after all he's been through . . ."

Mrs. Madison looks away. "No, of course not. Besides, he's one of ours." Her voice trails off as if she's talking to herself.

"Excuse me?"

"Eddie Proffit—Nothing. Never mind."

"You said he was one of yours. Mrs. Madison, did you have something to do with this challenge? You're not trying to influence my curriculum from behind the scenes—"

"I don't know what you mean. Maxwell West brought the challenge."

"I'm asking if you had *something to do with* this challenge."

"I did not. I went over the paperwork when Mr. West brought it in, but I certainly did not initiate it. I will say, however, that I'm not sorry it happened. It's not a book I'd choose." Mrs. Madison is splitting hairs, as they say. If Ms. Lloyd could see what I see, she would know she has her on the run. Adults are just like kids; get them in a pinch and they'll say anything. She's embarrassed. I'd have killed for information like that when I was alive.

Ruth Lloyd turns away. "I see. Well, I'll be sure to encourage Eddie to bring his copy back."

"I don't understand, Ruth. There are a thousand good books."

"And *Warren Peece* is one of them," Ruth says.

Mrs. Madison decides this is neither the time nor place. And she's right, because she has no idea how fast Ruth Lloyd would be in her face if she started a philosophical discussion about censorship now, principal or not. Ruth Lloyd is *steaming.*

"That's it, class," Ms. Lloyd says at the sound of the bell. "I'll see you all tomorrow. Eddie, could you stay a minute?"

Historically, when he's asked to stay after class it's trouble, but since he hasn't been talking, that particular kind of trouble has stayed at a distance. He drops his backpack and sits in the desk closest to Ms. Lloyd's.

"I've enjoyed you in class so far this year," she says to him, and he smiles. "Of course your silence has been a gift, if your reputation is even close to accurate," and he smiles again and nods. "But I'd rather have you talking, Eddie."

She steps forward and puts her hand on his shoulder. "I'm so sorry for all you've lost," she says. "I was at your father's funeral, and I know you stormed out because you loved him and because of how unfair it seemed and how much it hurt."

Eddie grits his teeth, but he can't stop the tear breaking the surface tension at the corner of his eye. "And then Billy," she says. What should bring a flood of tears actually brings a smile, but Ms. L misreads it; she thinks it's born of some small memory, when it's actually born of the knowledge that even when I die I don't go away.

"I have to say something, Eddie," she says. "I don't know whether or not it's appropriate, but it is something I care so much about. I don't need an answer; I just need to say it. It seems some of the kids have gotten their hands on copies of *Warren Peece* and finished it. Mrs. Madison accused me of providing it, and when I told her I confiscated all the books, except for yours, just as she instructed, she said, 'He's one of ours.' I don't know exactly what that means, but I assumed it meant you're in favor of removing the book. I would never tell a student what or how to think, but . . ."—and her eyes fill with tears—"I hope it's not true. I believe in stories, Eddie. I believe stories have the power to heal. I believe in ideas."

Eddie looks up and smiles. He smiles so bright that Ruth Lloyd can't take it wrong. He smiles so bright he might just as well say, "I believe in ideas, too, Ms. Lloyd, don't sweat it."

She's so worried about what she's thinking she misses Eddie's message. "I feel so bad for what you've been through," she says, "that I don't know how I could fight against you. I hope that doesn't happen, because I have to defend this book, and all books, like a warrior. I have to, Eddie. If you're on the other side, please know I'm just fighting for an idea, I'm not fighting against you, okay?"

Eddie stands and smiles even bigger. If he doesn't reel it in, his face is going to break. He places one hand on her shoulder as he reaches into his backpack and extracts the book. He pats it against his heart three times and holds it there. He says, "All done," and hands it to her.

Ms. Lloyd is dumbfounded a second, startled at the sound of Eddie's voice; but when she starts to speak, he puts his finger to his lips and shushes her. He winks and leaves.

In the hall Dan Moeltke catches up with him. "Hey, big guy. The school board meeting for the challenge on *Warren Peece* is coming up. You ready? Mr. Tarter is worried you may not start talking soon enough to help us. We need you, man. People will see you making connections again; they'll know you're coming back. Everyone is rooting for you, Eddie. This is the perfect time for you to speak out. You have a chance to make an impact."

Eddie grins. He'll be there. He'll be talking.

I butt out on Eddie's run this afternoon because I sense he wants to be alone. Actually I don't sense it, he *thinks* it, which in our relationship is like talking. He truly has the power to let me in or out, and he's beginning to recognize how that works. If I were alive, I'd be offended when he doesn't want to see me, because I could be a needy little bugger back then, but a good dose of death takes being offended away. It's really very nice being dead.

But I don't have to bump him to glide along and know everything he thinks: Man, why do they want to control your head? Jesus would of finished that book. He would of taken Chris Crutcher out for a McWine and McBread lunch after he read it, too. He would of underlined all the good parts and read 'em to his friends out in some corner of the playground.

Jesus was a tough guy. Didn't those guys READ those Bible lessons? Jesus wouldn't stop you from reading stuff; he'd talk to you after you did.

Eddie's legs pump hard as he moves into a slight hill, and he feels stronger with every stride. From now on, nobody takes *nothin'* from me. I'll read every book they try to get and buy every rap CD they put on their stupid little list. I might run Warren Peece for student body president.

The slap of his running shoes on the pavement quickens as he hardens his resolve. As always, the more stress on his body the clearer his thoughts. If Coach were smart he'd give Eddie a really hard math problem right before every race and offer him a Dixie Chicks CD if he could solve it by the end of the race. Eddie would be a world-record holder. Man, this story is going to have a great ending, even if everybody dies.

I know the deep reason Eddie struggles with the loss of Warren Peece and his fictional friends, and he does, too, though he doesn't know he knows it. He'll figure it out, though. It's because, even though they have really hard lives, harder than Eddie could imagine (at least before this year), they don't go away. He let himself fall in love with the characters in a book because they were safe. He knew they wouldn't die in the end because, for one thing, the story was being told by one of them. It seems as if everything he has allowed himself to love in this last year has been taken. And even though my reappearance has eased that a little, they ain't gettin' any more.

13

Something about the Author

I'm sitting on top of the furnace, which I don't recommend for living people, watching my dad read the last pages of *Warren Peece* to the "dregs" of Bear Creek High School. Ms. Lloyd stands in the back of the room, following along in her copy. It has to be ninety-five degrees in here, and not one kid is asleep. Good book.

"The end," Dad says, and slams the book shut. "We did it. We're gonna get in big trouble, but we did it." The room is filled over capacity. Word spread that the book no one was supposed to read was being read in the catacombs after school, and more kids showed every day.

There is a round of applause. Half the kids in this room have never finished a book.

"Tell you guys what. When the school board hearing comes around, it's not going to matter what the adults have to say. Most of our minds are made up, and all you have to do is walk into the supermarket to get our opinions. What will matter is what *you* say. Most of you know YFC is going to come out strong against the book. That group is made up of some of the best students and a few of the better athletes. I don't see that kind of star power in this room, no offense. If you guys are going to win this one, you're gonna have to do it with smarts."

I can feel the incredulity index increase tenfold. We're going to take on Dan Moeltke with brainpower??? bounces around the room like a Ping-Pong ball. That's like taking on Stephen Hawkings in *Jeopardy*, where all the categories are astrophysics. Actually I'm the only one who thinks that, but if I'm actually going to get this story published, I have to take some creative license.

"I can hear what you're thinking," Dad says, "but you're wrong. There's as much brainpower in this room as anywhere in the school. You guys have been listening too much to your own press."

"So how do we go about this?" Debbie Simmons asks. Debbie is a mousy girl who has probably read as many books as the rest of the kids in the room combined. Reading is about all Debbie does.

"You get organized," Dad says. "You get a statement drawn up, and you choose someone to deliver it. Someone with flair. Someone who isn't afraid to stand up to Dan Moeltke in a debate."

Montana West's eyes light up. "I'll read it," she says. "Oh, jeez, Mr. Bartholomew, let me read it. Wouldn't that be so cool? Have my dad get up there and say all the crap he's going to say, then I'll come right behind him telling the whole school board how he's so full of—"

"Let us use our imaginations on how that sentence ends," Dad says. "Anyone have a problem with Montana reading your statement?"

Montana West is unanimously elected reader of the nonreaders' statement.

"And Montana," Dad says as the group is breaking up, "might I suggest that no matter what you think your father is full of, if it's in any way scatological, delete it. Remember, people, they'll be looking for reasons to discount what you have to say. Three of the board members are also members of the Red Brick Church board. That puts you at a decided disadvantage."

Like I said before, if you were going to call up the perfect prototype for the daughter Maxwell West did not order, Montana is the one you'd come up with. Goth kids call her Goth. Black clothes, enough chains to start a towing company. One of many tattoos she got with her fake ID is a bird pulling a worm out of her belly button. Her preferred reading list is made up entirely of graphic novels, her idea of the perfect dreamboat is Donnie Darko, and though she played connect-the-dots all over her last IQ test with black crayon, she's smarter than they get. She knows KOЯN so well she can sing all their songs backward. She is also *way* decent when it comes to people who are like I used to be. She'll see somebody sitting alone in the lunchroom and just go over and sit down and start a conversation, like that person matters as much as Dan Moeltke. When she talks to you, you just light up.

But pick a conversation, any conversation, between Montana and Maxwell, and you get something like this.

"You're not going out like that, young lady."

"Like what?"

"Dressed like the devil himself."

"The devil doesn't look like this, Maxwell. The devil wears a red suit and has horns and a three-pronged pitchfork. I'm dressed more like your standard small-time cult follower. Or a school shooter."

"Don't you be disrespectful with me, young lady. I am your father, not 'Maxwell.' You will address me as such."

"I won't be disrespectful if you won't be disrespectful."

"What's that supposed to mean? What have you done lately that deserves respect?"

"Well, let's see. I have a three-point-seven-nine grade point average. I made the debate team last year. I got my driver's license and I haven't wrecked the car hardly at all—"

"What?!"

"Just kidding, Maxwell. I haven't wrecked it at all."

"And you do nothing but embarrass me. You are not going out with all those piercings, looking like some lady of the evening."

"You mean like a prostitute?"

"Yes, I mean like a prostitute."

Montana goes to the living-room mirror and strikes a pose. "You really think so, Maxwell? How much do you think I'd go for?"

"You little trollop. You get to your room, you're not going anywhere tonight. You will learn to respect the rules in my house, or you will suffer the consequences."

Montana keeps baiting him, and Mr. West gets madder and madder until he's ready to strike her, and then she moves right into his face and says, "Go ahead, Maxwell. Then I'll turn the other cheek and you can hit that one, too," and it usually stops. One time it didn't, which is why Montana is able to get away with it. Maxwell West was so horrified that he struck his daughter in the face, albeit with an open hand, that she sometimes gets away with murder. It was the day after that incident that she got the worm tattoo. A good whack carries with it a lot of capital.

They love each other; I mean, if one of them died, the other one would be *way* sorry, but neither expects the other one to do that soon, so they fight like gladiators. Tell you what, Maxwell West is a smart guy, but if I were he (dead guys know good grammar), the one person I'd stay out of a verbal squabble with is his daughter.

"Okay, time to get down to the truth. Billy Bartholomew, is this really you?

"O ye of little faith. You need to hear more Russian?"

"How crazy does this make me?"

"No crazier than you already were."

"I need to know all I can know," Eddie says.

"Ask and ye shall receive."

"Was that you on the courthouse lawn telling me to come in out of the rain?

"In the flesh," I tell him. "Well, in the spirit."

"So I wasn't crazy."

"Well, you did run out into the stormy night in your pajama bottoms with no shoes on."

"You know what I mean."

He runs, letting me sink in, allowing himself to believe a little, then a little more. And I feel the moment his faith kicks in. He's been close before, but now he simply decides it doesn't matter if I'm "real" or not. I'm there, he's talking to me, case closed. He says, "Why did you come back?"

"Actually, I never left, but I'm here because of you. You're my friend, and you'll always be my friend. We're connected into eternity. Dead or alive. I didn't want you to waste the rest of your teenage years brooding and grieving and wondering why just because two of the people you cared about most were too absentminded to stay in the game. And I wanted you to know everything turns out okay, so you don't have to be afraid, and you can do what you need to do whenever you need to do it."

"I really don't like you being so confident and everything," he says. "That's all backward."

He runs farther, speeding up, working for that clarity. "I can't figure out exactly why the book thing is so important to me."

"Want me to tell you?"

"Uh-huh."

"Because it's about freedom. A guy out there writes a story and it moves your teacher and she decides to see if it moves the kids. It does; some, anyway. It's not a classic; it's not a Bible, but it's a story told by a guy who wants to get his little piece of truth out there. You recognize it, you feel the connection, and then somebody tries to take it away from you. So you get hacked off because they're messing with your freedom. It could be any book, you know. Freedom is a birthright."

"Do you know Chris Crutcher? I mean, now that you're dead?"

"I know anybody I want to know."

"What's he like? I mean, what would he think about all this?"

"He'd love it. It happens a lot, and even though

he's an old guy, he's kind of arrested in his teenage years. Likes a good fight. He was a lot like you in school; had a hard time paying attention and was in trouble a lot for opening his mouth without raising his hand or thinking. He isn't as smart as you are, and not as spiritual. He could never connect to me like this, but he could connect to you. Takes him forever to write a book because every thought leads to a whole bunch of other thoughts that have nothing to do with the story he's telling. But he finally gets them out there."

"So he's worth fighting for?" Eddie says. He's running easy now, in that zone where he could run forever. I'm glad I'm dead and just floating beside him, because if I were alive I'd be into third-degree oxygen debt.

"This isn't about him, Eddie. You know that. Chris Crutchers are a dime a dozen. And it's only a little bit about you. Heck, you've already read the book. It's about freedom, with a little 'f.' You live in a free country, at

least relatively speaking. I can go back into the heads of the people who created it, and what I can tell you is that they wanted the little freedoms, the ones that affected them in the moment. It's easy to go back in history books and look at the big picture, see the larger philosophies and all that. But people do things in their regular lives that affect them right then. The big stuff is little and the little stuff is big. If you don't make your stand here, you'll make it later, you're wired that way, but there will always be people who are afraid, who will try to take your freedom. They'll tell you what to be afraid of and how to be afraid, and they'll tell you if you follow them they'll keep you safe."

"But I won't be safe, will I?"

"You got it, buddy."

"I'll always be scared, because I'll be waiting around for them to tell me what else to be afraid of. Like Tarter and the YFC want everyone to be afraid of Warren Peece.*"*

"Right. If you let them take this one thing away, you

give them the right to take everything. It's about freedom, man."

Eddie stops and turns toward me—I mean directly toward me, though I only weigh twenty-one grams and can't be seen. He knows exactly where I am. "Are you going to stay with me?" he asks.

"Not much longer."

His shoulders slump.

"You won't need me," I tell him. "You're way farther along than I am, Eddie. I won't leave until you say it's okay, how about that?"

"Promise?"

"Promise," I say back. "Everything's under your control. Actually that's true for everyone; most people just don't know it.

He starts running again. "Tell me about Tarter," he says.

"He's not nearly as scary as we thought," I say back. "Tell you this, he's never done anything to anyone half as tough as was done to him. Relatively speaking, he's

evolving nicely. Just remember: He's scared and he can't afford for anyone to see that. He's not the enemy. His ideas are the enemy. He's doing his best."

"So I should be nice to him?"

"Be however you need to be to do what feels right. He signed up for the game, too, and it's not your job to make his game easier. Your job is to tell your truth. That's everybody's job."

"Even Chris Crutcher?"

"Yeah, he's doing his best, too. I said, he's not as smart as you."

For a moment I hear only the even slap of his shoes on the dusty trail and the rhythm of his breathing. "Is he scared, too?"

"He's scared, too. But he's not scared to tell his stories. That's probably the only place he's not scared."

• • •

To: Stotan717@aol.com

From: Nonproffit14@hotmail.com

Dear Mr. Crutcher,

My name is Eddie Proffit. I found your e-mail address at your website and thought I would take a chance and see if you would answer me back, though I'm sure you're way too busy. Our class was assigned to read your really good book, *Warren Peece,* and everybody loved it. Well, almost everybody. One of the teachers in our school is a Christian guy who doesn't think there should be bad language in a book or that it should talk about religion or abortion or people disobeying their parents. He also thinks it's bad to make gay people look good in stories because he thinks it might make people want to be gay. So some people in his church lodged a formal complaint to make us stop reading *Warren Peece* and also to take all your other books out of our library. Our librarian, Ms. Lloyd, is getting ready to commit mass murder because of all this, and they are going to have a school board meeting to see if they can keep your books banned. I was wondering if you could maybe write something down to me in an e-mail that I could read at the meeting. Maybe the school board would wake up if the author said something.

By the way, I live in Bear Creek, Idaho, and my dad and my best friend died within three months of each other and I was the first one to find both of them so it hasn't been all that great of a year. It would make me feel a whole lot better if I could, like, deliver a knockout punch on this Christian guy who is also a preacher and who keeps on wanting me to get baptized so God will stop doing mean things to me, which isn't what's really happening. Thanks in advance in case you decide to send me something.

Eddie Proffit

A response comes back almost immediately—Crutcher is sitting at his computer trying to write a coherent opening sentence for his next book, already overdue, when Eddie's e-mail comes in—with a message for Eddie to read at the school board meeting, "when you think the time is appropriate," along with condolences for his hard year. He includes some other ideas to make the school board meeting rock. Eddie pumps a fist into the air, prints the e-mail, folds it neatly, and slips it into his back pocket.

14

If the Game's Too Easy . . .

What I told Eddie about the Reverend Tarter is true. I would have shown him this, but it wouldn't be fair to give Eddie a look inside the place where the fear comes from in Tarter's life. A human being is not born as rigid and afraid as Sanford Tarter. Life teaches those things. I bounce into seven-year-old Sandy Tarter's life moments after his mother has caught him playing with matches. She grips his left hand by the wrist, holds a lighter close to his fingers, threatening to show him what fire can do to flesh.

"Please, Momma!" he screams. "Please don't burn me! I'm sorry! I won't do it again!"

His mother brings the lighter closer. "You better pray to Jesus, little boy. You better pray to Jesus. He is the only one who can stop these little fingers from being burned black."

"Please, Momma!"

"Quit your whining!"

"Momma—"

"PRAY TO JESUS!"

"Please, Jesus, please don't let me get burned. I'll never do it again, Jesus. I promise! I'll never play with matches again!"

"Get on your knees!"

Sandy Tarter drops to his knees and closes his eyes, convulsing, begging Jesus to spare him.

His mother drops his hand, falls to her knees beside him, and begins to pray. "Dear Jesus, me and my little boy . . ."

I can pop into little Sandy's life just about any

time I please to watch his mouth washed out with soap, vinegar, Tabasco sauce, or water from an unflushed toilet, though I don't necessarily care to. The only thing I want my friend Eddie Proffit to know is what I already said—that Sanford Tarter has never, in his years of teaching or his years of preaching, even approached leveling the fear on a student or a parishioner that was leveled on him.

If humans are ever to understand one another, they will have to come to terms with the concept, and the reality, of relativity. In essence, that's what the Earthgame is about. They will have to see how things look compared to other things. Once you understand that nothing exists without its opposite, you understand nothing is good and nothing is evil, that opposites actually hold each other up. For instance, if Ms. Lloyd and Mr. Tarter could see what I see, they might have a lot more to say to each other and might come to an easy agreement about this censorship issue and the nature of kids in general. Authors aren't good or evil. Most tell their stories the best way they can. Stories aren't good or evil either; they're just reflections of one person's perception of the world. One kid might read that story and feel recognized, might find a connection. Another kid might read the same story and be offended or angered or bored. If those two students got together and talked about their reactions to the story, they'd know each other a little better.

But that's the game. The game would be too easy if we understood, and maybe no one would want to play.

Eddie walks into Mr. Tarter's classroom after school on the Friday before the Tuesday school board meeting. Tarter is nearly incapable of appearing eager to talk with anyone. Eddie waits.

"Could I speak to you for a moment, sir?" Eddie says.

Tarter registers exactly zero surprise at the sound of Eddie's voice. "Of course, Edward. What can I do for you?"

"I'd like to do my testimony this Sunday if possible. I've finished the workbooks and written the essay. I think the only requirement I have left is the testimony itself."

"It's a little short notice—"

"I know, but if I'm going to talk at the school board meeting, it's probably best that I talk somewhere else first; you know, get used to it. Besides, that will make me a member of YFC, which should add to the weight of what I say."

"What I've been saying all along, Edward. I guess you've been listening. You had me worried." Tarter smiles. "I can set it up right before the offering. Actually, they might give more right after they hear you talk for the first time. I'm kidding, of course."

"I know," Eddie says. "Thanks. I need to get going if I'm gonna get both my presentation for church and for the school board done."

"Godspeed," Tarter says, and as Eddie reaches the door, "Edward, I'd like to see a copy of your testimony before you actually give it, if possible. Can you get that to me?"

"I think so," Eddie says back. "If I don't get it done tomorrow, I'll bring it on Sunday morning."

"I suppose I can follow along," Tarter says. "I've seen your class work, so I'm sure your testimony will be on the mark."

Right on the mark of Cain, Eddie thinks, but he says, "Yes, sir."

"Aren't you supposed to be in class?"

I'm watching my dad take his tools off the hooks on the wall and place them carefully into his toolbox when Eddie shows up. "Yup," he says. "I'm supposed to be in Ms. Lloyd's class. She let me out to go to the can. You got a can down here?"

"No, but I *got* canned."

"Ms. Lloyd told us. That really sucks. For the readings, huh?"

"For the readings," Dad says.

"Ms. Lloyd's really upset," Eddie says. "She's up there ranting like a crazy woman."

"You go back up there and tell her not to let a soul know she was present for any of it. They're looking for any reason they can find to get rid of disloyal opposition. Her head could already be on the chopping block. I only read the last few chapters; *she* brought the book into the school in the first place. She's the dangerous one."

"What are you going to do? Most of the kids in class want to boycott school."

"Don't you guys be doing that. I'll lay low for a while and see if I can get my job back. I'll let that codger they brought in to replace me try to figure out this antiquated, jury-rigged heating system, and the bell system and the snow removal equipment and what-all. A few weeks of that ought to soften them up a little."

"You should sabotage some stuff on your way out."

"Don't think I didn't consider it; the Eddie Proffit

in me is popping out all over. But I don't think it will be necessary. That guy was staring at the *fuse box* like it came from NASA."

"You got enough money and everything? Food?"

Dad smiles. "Hey, Eddie, don't you worry about me. I have savings and I have Billy's entire college fund to squander. I'm fine."

"Man, this sucks. They're firing a guy from a school for reading to kids."

"If they don't stop me, the terrorists win," Dad says. My dad's pretty funny.

"Hey, listen," Eddie says. "What are you doing this Sunday?"

Dad's eyes narrow. "I don't know," he says. "What am I doing this Sunday?"

"You're coming to the Red Brick Church to hear me testify," Eddie says.

Dad laughs and shakes his head. "Now that," he says, "I'm going to enjoy."

"I just hope I can keep my mind on track," Eddie

says. "I've been practicing in my room, and every time I give it, it turns out different."

"How different?" Dad says.

"Way different," Eddie says back, "if I start thinking too much while I'm talking. You know me, Mr. Bartholomew."

"After the formal challenge," Dan Moeltke says to the full assembly of the Youth for Christ, "Mr. West will get to talk, and then Ms. Lloyd will rebut. Then the floor is open to the public. As a group, we want to hit the same points again and again, like politicians do. You all have speaking points; memorize them. Use these words as much as you can: 'obscene,' 'disrespectful,' 'immoral,' 'irrelevant.' The more often they hear them the better they'll stick. Make up your own testimony, and work the words in as naturally as you can, but in the end we want them to know it is offensive for us to have to read this kind of language in a school assignment, that we believe the issues portrayed are un-Christian and that we shouldn't have to be exposed to homosexuality, abortion, masturbation, and all that. Those are issues that need to be taken up with people of our own faith, and those people are our families."

I think I'll stand up and say I have faith in masturbation, Eddie thinks. I could bump him right now and say he *must* have faith in it, as often as he turns to it, but I don't want him to start giggling for no reason. It will take a Herculean effort on his part to keep his mouth shut long enough to accomplish all he has in mind. He thinks about his dad. He believes John Proffit would be proud if he pulls this off. He thinks about his mom. He goes back to thinking about his dad.

"I'll go first to set the agenda, then the rest of you get in among the townspeople. Don't line up together, because we want to break up those against banning *Warren Peece* and not let them get a run of five or six." He points to Eddie. "Then our rising star will bring it to a close."

Eddie smiles and takes a bow.

"Nobody has heard Eddie talk for almost four months. He'll be testifying for his baptism on Sunday, but only church members will hear him. People may know he talked, but the school board meeting will be the first time they actually hear him."

"Honey?" Eddie's mother says. She's standing in the doorway to his room.

Eddie looks up from his desk.

"I'm really glad you've decided to open up. And I'm so relieved you're coming into the church. It's been a source of great solace to me. I can truly say that the church saved my life. I loved your father, I truly did, but it was such a struggle fighting his beliefs. He was a good man, but he was misguided. I sometimes wonder if—"

He knows he's in danger of blowing his cover, but Eddie can't help himself. "He didn't die because of his beliefs, Mom. He died because he forgot to let the air out of a truck tire before breaking it down."

"But if . . . the Reverend Tarter has said—"

"Could we let it go, Mom?"

"I'm really glad you came into the church," she says.

"Can't you haunt her or something?" Eddie asks me when his bedroom door closes behind his mother.

"I don't know," I say. "I've never tried anything like that."

"You haunted me.*"*

"You *haunted you," I say back. "That ghoul you saw was never me."*

That's the one thing Eddie's still not sure of. He thinks I haunted him to get him to notice me. I have to admit it's what I would have done when I was alive, which is Catch-22 all over the place, because if I were alive, I couldn't *have haunted him. "Man," he says, "what am I going to do with her?"*

"Want me to tell you?"

"I asked, didn't I?"

"You're gonna go right on ahead and outgrow her. She'll either catch up or not. Might help you to remember that out here, sometimes the old look young and the young look old."

"Tell you one thing," he says.

"What?"

"I liked it a lot better when you were alive and I ran things."

I laugh. "You still run things, Eddie. Don't ever sweat that."

15

Unedited Testimony

I accompany Eddie and his mom and my dad through the church parking lot the Sunday before the school board hearing on *Warren Peece.* We pass bumper stickers reading BEAR CREEK CITIZENS FOR RESPONSIBLE CURRICULUM and PABBIS (which stands for Parents Against Bad Books In Schools—a national organization). Eddie's mom seems uneasy about having Dad with them, particularly because he's carrying a large cloth book bag, but Eddie told her he wanted Dad there, and she wasn't up for an argument.

At the door, a church elder tells Dad he can attend the regular service, but when Eddie begins to testify, only members are allowed; church policy. Dad protests, but it is written in stone. Eddie is their secret weapon, and they're not about to unveil him until the board hearing.

It is a fiery sermon by Earth standards. The Reverend Tarter is never better than when he has an immediate cause, and saving Bear Creek's youngsters falls right into that category.

"Ladies and gentlemen," he says after the first hymn, "our town is at a crossroads. We are in a fight for the hearts, minds, and souls of our children. Make no mistake about it: We are in a battle, nay; might I say we are at war. It is a righteous war, however, and if we win no one will lose.

"I am instituting a draft to fight this war; a draft for Christian soldiers. There won't be a lottery for this draft, because you all draw number one. We need each and every one of you.

"Basic philosophies are at odds, friends. No clearer lines have been drawn between good and evil. The books of Chris Crutcher and authors like him are written to influence our children, particularly our teens, in a way that is completely unacceptable. It is time for grown-ups with Christian values, whether they have children or not, to stand against words and ideas that poison young minds. Tomorrow night we will meet *en masse* at the high-school gym for the school board meeting to rid the school of *Warren Peece*, but that is just the beginning. Before this war is over, the entire curriculum of our school, K to 12 will be reviewed, and the administrators and teachers will justify their decisions or make different ones. We are a powerful force in this community, with true watchdog power.

"The issues dealt with in *Warren Peece* are to be dealt with in the home, under the watchful eye of concerned and informed parents. They are not to be left to teachers who may or may not have the sensibilities to deal with them, and who certainly do not share your and my concerns about our children."

You could say he's preaching to the choir (and you'd be right in a literal sense), but the entire congregation hangs on his every word. You can *feel* them rising to the occasion. At least I can. Tarter outlines his objections, focusing on the homosexual character and the "disrespectful" language. He calls the book blasphemous. He calls Chris Crutcher blasphemous. He calls "the person who brought the book into our school, decent as she may be," blasphemous.

"My friends, I hold the author of this book no ill will. He will have to make his peace with the Lord in due time, and while I'd certainly like to be there for his explanation, in the end that is between him and God. He doesn't even know the children to whom he does this spiritual damage. But our business is here and now, and it is up to us to stop this country, school by school, town by town, from this dark spiral toward evil."

If he weren't there to support Eddie as far as he can, my dad would get up and leave, maybe holler a few choice words of his own truth on the way out. I can *feel* him seething. Eddie's mom is sitting in the choir, so Dad and Eddie are alone together. Eddie leans over and whispers, "If you're gonna throw up or something, it would be okay if you leave now."

Dad chuckles and whispers back. "In World War Two, when bombers had to go deep into Germany, they had fighter escorts for as far as the fighters could go and still get back safely. Then they'd come back and meet them on the way back. I can't go all the way with you, but I'll be here when you're done." He nods to the book bag on the floor. "Wish I could go all the way."

The book bag is full of cue cards. Dad was going to stand at the back of the congregation and hold them up to keep Eddie's bouncing brain in the groove.

"I'm trying to picture them in order," Eddie says,

"but it isn't working. Every time Tarter says something, I think of something I should say back. I'm not really very good at this."

"I know," Dad says. "What do you want to do?"

"Guess I'll have to wing it," Eddie whispers. He smiles. "Pray for me."

". . . what Jesus would do," the reverend continues. "I know it's a cliché. They laugh at us for asking the question, but it is a Christian's job to shrug off the barbs of the unfaithful and answer the tough questions. What Jesus would do is go to that meeting and stand up for our children. Jesus would say to the school board what we all know, that evil lurks in every corner, disguises itself in any possible way, even in the cloak of a children's writer. Evil has no conscience, none.

"Jesus would do what *our* young people are doing," and he points to the section roped off for Youth for Christ. "Jesus would bring like-minded people, his followers and his flock, and face this evil down." Tarter mops his brow lightly with a handkerchief. "This is our chance not only to talk like Christians but to walk like Christians. We must keep our eye on our goal and march toward it as Jesus marched toward Calvary. I'm asking each of you to attend that school board meeting tomorrow night. It will be held in the school gymnasium at seven o'clock. Do not stay home if you don't have children in school. You have a responsibility not only to yourselves but to all other community members."

I hear some serious "amens."

The reverend pauses and backs off a little. "After the final hymn, we will welcome a special young man into our church; a boy who has suffered much over the past year, but who is now finding the solid ground of his faith. I hope you all will stay to welcome Edward Proffit."

Eddie looks over at the choir box and sees pride spread across his mother's face. He feels a twinge of regret because he's pretty sure that pride will be followed by tears when she hears what he has to say, but he figures as mad or as hurt or as disappointed as she'll be, things would be a lot worse in the long run if he went ahead and did what she wants him to do. Because he would always resent her. He knows I'm right. She needs to take care of herself.

When the final chord of "The Old Rugged Cross" fades, Tarter motions Eddie to the front of the room, as he respectfully asks anyone who is not a church member to leave; this ceremony is for only the faithful. Dad rises and discreetly walks up a side aisle. Eddie's running his testimony over in his head, but he can already feel it slipping away with the book bag.

As Tarter introduces him, recounting specifically all he's been through over the past year, including his being "struck dumb," Eddie concentrates harder on his message and his heart begins to pound and I see the window, opening exactly as it does when he is starting a run. And I know this about the universe.

If the window is there, it is there to go through, which I do.

Now the only time Eddie has actually *seen* me is in a dream. That's no big trick, because he remembers what I look like. The rest of the time he just sort of *feels* me beside him. But I gotta get seriously visible now, and I need to get it *right*.

Eddie looks above the congregation at the huge triple doors leading to the outer foyer, and what he sees is his old friend yours truly, standing atop Summer's Hill in my snowsuit and my stupid Russian hat with the earmuffs, holding my daddy's cue cards. Eddie actually smiles and waves, which causes the entire congregation to turn 180 degrees to stare at the door. He steps to the pulpit, the same pulpit from which the Reverend Tarter just delivered his lode. Eddie is intimidated, more than he thought he'd be. He gazes into the faces of the congregation, and his throat clogs. He sees me waving above them and focuses on the first card, which just says TALK. "I'm nervous," he says. "It's been a long time since I've said anything. But the testimonial classes I've been taking have prepared me, I think." He takes a breath, looks at the next card, which reads LIFE, JESUS.

"It's a scary step to give your life to the Lord, because it means you have to just give up and have faith that he'll know what to do with it when he gets it."

Many in the congregation nod and smile slightly.

"When you think of all the people in the world who are doing that, he must be pretty busy. You get worried he won't handle yours right. But then you ask Reverend Tarter, and he reminds you who Jesus is, and you relax."

Eddie leans forward on the pulpit, gripping it at the sides. He looks up and sees the word DAD on my next card. "Everybody here knows my dad died last year," he says. "I don't know whether you know this part or not, but my dad and Reverend Tarter didn't see things the same way. I used to listen to them argue down at the service station, and when they were done I'd ask Dad how anybody was supposed to figure out which one of them was right."

There is a silence, like the congregation is waiting for Eddie Proffit to say Tarter was right and his dad was wrong. My next cue card wasn't in Dad's book bag. I make it on the spot, because dead guys can do that, and I hold it up high. It says DO IT!

"My dad said, 'Do the numbers, Eddie. Do science and the numbers.' "

He looks up at the next card and sees LEVITICUS and takes a deep breath. If he goes here, he passes the point of no return. His mind bounces now, but it bounces the way he wishes it would always bounce: from cause to effect, though those probably aren't the words he'd use.

He sees Leviticus the way he pictures him from

reading the Bible: vastly unpleasant. He sees Matthew Shepard hanging on a fence in Laramie, Wyoming, because, and only because, he was gay. His mind jumps to fire hoses pointed at black people in the sixties, a bomb explosion in a small church in Birmingham, Alabama, and he remembers what Reverend Tarter said about the mark of Cain. He does the math. About ten percent of Americans are African American. About ten percent of Americans are homosexual. Nobody chose it. It's the math. God created the math.

"One thing you do when you're getting ready to testify is read as much of the Bible as you can understand, because you know the stuff that's in there is supposed to tell you how to live your life, and that's also why you take the class, so you'll have somebody to ask about the parts you don't get. Like if you believe in statistics, approximately one person out of every ten is gay. The baptism classes tell you that's a sin. Like, a big one. There's this guy named Leviticus in the Old Testament who says if you do what gay people do, you are an abomination. There aren't many things worse than an abomination."

The congregation is beginning to wonder if they're about to experience something very different from your run-of-the-mill testimony.

"Only what if you *are* gay?"

Tarter registers his first signs of discontent. Eddie waited until the last minute to give him the text outline, and now Tarter starts to thumb ahead. From his chair to the side, he whispers, "Get on task, Eddie."

Eddie hears him. Tarter doesn't realize the last thing he wants is for Eddie to get on task.

"If you are, it means you can't ever have sex your whole life. Because if you're gay, you aren't going to *want* to have sex with the opposite sex and you can't have it with the same sex, because Leviticus is the kind of guy who goes for the maximum punishment. He says, 'the land will spue you out,' which . . . I'm not sure exactly what that means, but it sounds radical. See, and this is where my dad comes in. Science and math, remember? Ten percent. It's always been ten percent, even when Leviticus was alive. Now you know it can't be hereditary, because that would mean gay people would beget other gay people and most gay people don't beget, so there would be this serious drop in gay people. It's just ten percent at *random*. If being gay was really a sin, that would mean that God went and created one out of every ten people and made it a sin for them to have sex, *for their whole lives.* I hear over and over and over how God is a loving God. Now I could see where that could be a little bit funny if it were only for a few weeks or something, but not for your *whole life.* So I figure Leviticus was just a bigoted guy, just like whoever the guy was that decided the mark of Cain was being black. And I'm thinking I like girls, see, but there wasn't this day when I woke up and said,

'I think I'll like girls.' I just did. So I figure it has to be the same way with being gay. You wake up one morning and you say, 'I like boys,' only you *are* a boy. If you had a choice, why would you choose that? So you could get called names and beat up more in school? Just because information is church information doesn't mean it shouldn't include common sense, should it?"

I'm still there if he needs me, but Eddie's not checking me out above the door anymore, so I'm checking out the crowd to see if there's going to be, like, a *backlash* or something, because some really big loggers and ranchers are getting restless. I hold up the card that says CHURCH BUSINESS/SCHOOL BUSINESS, hoping maybe he'll glance up.

"Speaking of school," Eddie says, nodding at me so I know he felt the bump, "I know the people in this church all want to ban the book *Warren Peece*, and you're going to the school board meeting to say so. I think it's pretty clear from what I've said so far that my baptism is postponed indefinitely, so this is probably my last Sunday here, but I'll be at school every day for the next four years. I'd like to make a deal with you. I won't come here and bring my school business, and you don't come there and bring your church business."

Mr. Tarter rises and moves slowly toward Eddie, but when Eddie sees him he backs away. "Guess I better wrap this up," he says. "But man, I've got so much more to testify to."

Tarter motions for two church elders to move in on Eddie from the sides. Eddie steps toward the crowd to avoid them, but two larger members of the congregation move in from there. No escape.

Tarter moves faster. You can almost see his pulse in his neck from across the room. In fact if you're me, you can. The Reverend Tarter has a healthy heartbeat.

Eddie glances around, sees himself closed in on all sides, but all his fear is gone. He looks up at the cue cards where I have written RUN FOR IT. Behind him, ten feet above the pulpit, is a huge stained-glass window with a picture of the Virgin Mary backed by a white halo, and below that window is a ledge. Eddie runs directly at the congregation, reverses direction three inches from two elders' outstretched fingers, and sprints past the pulpit; jumps, curls his fingers over the window ledge, pulls himself up far enough to get a grip on the handle at the bottom of the window, and pulls himself the rest of the way. He stands, looking down. The sun shines through the window, through the Virgin Mary's halo, and makes a perfect aura around Eddie Proffit.

Most of the men trying to get to him are too out of shape to pull themselves onto the ledge. Maxwell West, the most athletic, falls back to the floor when Eddie steps on his fingers.

The next card says JESUS.

"About Jesus," he says. "What *would* Jesus do? I've read that book you are all supposed to help get rid of because of how it's going to mess up our minds. Then I look around at all the people who like the book, and the ones who like it most are the ones who never get anything from our school and they never get anything from here either. They aren't cool. You know who they are? They're 'the least of my brethren.' So the minute I say, 'What would Jesus do?' I know the answer. He'd do what Billy's dad and Ms. Lloyd did. He'd give this book to people and read it to people, because Jesus was a guy who liked to make people feel better and that book makes some people feel better. So there."

If I still had any influence, I would remind my friend that "So there" is probably not testimonial material.

Tarter motions to Mrs. Alexander, the church organist, but her eyes are riveted to Eddie, who looks seriously like an angel up there with the Virgin Mary's halo around his head.

"Man," Eddie says, "the school *janitor* takes a

chance because he *does* like these kids and because he wants to do something nice for somebody after his own kid is gone, and he just finishes reading the book to them. That's all he does. He finishes reading the book. The school janitor did what Jesus would do. He read to the least of his brethren. And for that he gets fired. If Jesus is smart, he won't be coming back soon."

Eddie's about to get off task. I've got WRAP IT UP on the next card, but he is not looking.

"And you know what? If Jesus did come back today, like everybody in this church thinks he will before they die, nobody would listen to him. Jesus would do what Jesus would do and you'd just think he was another Mr. Bartholomew. I mean, think about Jesus. I've been reading all about him. He was a rebel. He would be right up here with me, telling you guys that kids can think for themselves and it's okay for them to read about hard things.

"In fact I might *be* Jesus. What about that? I

might be Jesus. If you read the Bible Cliff Notes, you know that when he was young, he didn't even know he was Jesus. I mean, he knew his name was that, but he didn't know he was the Christ for sure. There were a whole bunch of things he had to do before he could be the Christ, which is a title and not a name, by the way, so you can use it in vain."

I see Eddie's mom in the choir stall, looking on in horror. She does *not* want to have to explain to the congregation how her son thinks he's Jesus.

"Like, he had to stay out in the desert forty days and forty nights, which is a way long time if you've ever been to the desert. So he had to prove himself. And if he wouldn't of, then he wouldn't of been Jesus Christ and somebody else would of had to come along and do it. And now somebody has to come along and do it again. So maybe it's me. Maybe I haven't proved myself yet. Maybe one of the things I had to do was get up here out of your reach and yell at you and tell you that stupid book is okay, and why don't you leave us alone."

The Reverend Tarter has physically moved Mrs. Alexander to the organ, and she mercifully begins pounding out a really upbeat version of "The Church in the Valley by the Wildwood" and all of a sudden you can't hear Eddie Proffit anymore, but you can see his mouth moving, and I retire the cue cards completely and the church custodian is bringing the ladder, and this sermon on the ledge is about over.

The ladder comes up and Eddie comes down, sticks out his hands as if in surrender, and when the elders relax, he bolts for the door, is down the sidewalk, down the street, and gone.

16

How to Prepare Your School for an Author Visit

The parking lot to the American Legion Hall is full by six thirty on Monday evening. The hearing starts at seven thirty. Bumper stickers in this lot are a little more evenly matched, one side sporting I READ BANNED BOOKS and INTELLECTUAL FREEDOM ROCKS and the other side declaring exactly how many men and women it takes to make a real marriage (one of each), next to the word *Jesus* inside the outline of a fish. There is a heaviness in the air. People have been arguing in the supermarket and the drugstore. One fistfight broke out in the sawmill parking lot.

Most folks with differing opinions cannot talk about it civilly and have agreed not to try. Tonight, they have a forum. My friend Eddie Proffit isn't present because he is in the one room at the county hospital reserved for mental-health patients. It was the Jesus thing. Though he was only seen as hysterical for leaping up in front of the Virgin Mary, his "I might be Jesus" speech as related by Reverend Tarter seemed problematic to the mental-health professional, who has been on the job only a week and a half and was therefore susceptible to Tarter's concerns about Eddie's "delusions of grandeur." Eddie's mom was easy to convince because she has become more and more accustomed to the worst thing happening and Tarter's idea that the devil got inside Eddie sounded about right. Eddie told her she is going to feel really stupid when he comes out evaluated sane while everybody in the Red Brick Church is paranoid schizophrenic. He also called my dad to tell him what surprise to expect at the meeting on Monday. When he heard, I thought my dad would run up there and kiss him.

"Think they let you run cross country if you have a diagnosis?" Eddie asks me from his hospital bed. He's operating the motorized adjustment mechanism, raising his head, then his legs, then both.

"Want me to go find out?"

"Sure," he says. "I got time."

"They've never had reason to make a decision one way or the other," I tell him, "but there's no written rule against it."

"How do you know that? I thought you were gonna go find out."

"I did. Dead guys waste no time. In fact, there's no such thing."

"Man," he says, "I sure hate to miss that meeting."

"Won't matter," I say back. "Fifteen minutes after

church yesterday, your message was out. No sense being redundant."

"Yeah, well, go check it out and report back," he says. "I wanna know if they like my little surprise."

A buzz emanates from the American Legion Hall as the start time approaches. Almost everybody here knows Eddie went bananas in church over the censorship issue, but what most of them really heard is that he thinks he might be Jesus. The YFC kids sit together near the front, while most of my dad's furnace-room crew is grouped off to the side. Hundreds of adults fill the rest of the seats.

Mr. Northcutt, the school board chair, speaks. "The board has been here since seven," he says, "and has taken care of our other business so we can focus exclusively on the curriculum issues at hand." He reads the protest directly from the paperwork turned in by Maxwell West, who is not elected to the board yet but plans to be, and who has a seat at the board's table because he is lodging the protest. Ms. Lloyd is also there, as the primary person opposing the challenge. She is both dressed and fit to kill.

When Mr. Northcutt finishes reading the formal challenge, he turns over the floor to Maxwell West. Maxwell reiterates what is in the formal statement, then, "We are at a moral crossroads in our nation's and our community's schools, and as parents and responsible adults it is time to turn and stand our ground. From school shootings, to allowing provocative language and dress, to passing out condoms, to banning God from our children's education, we are simply falling into an abyss. It is simply immoral to stand by and do nothing." He speaks in a calm, reasonable tone. Max West is a pretty popular guy, even though plenty of folks don't agree with what sometimes seem like rigid views. He's a go-to guy when a community member dies or is hit by catastrophe, whether that person is a church member or not.

"The material in the book in question, *Warren Peece,* plainly and simply takes our children further down that path. It is time to let morality and common sense take over, and common sense tells me it is foolish to allow poison into our children's minds." He makes his point twice more, and sits.

When it's her turn, Ms. Lloyd stands, leaning straight armed on the table, addressing the board first directly. "I've loved books all my life," she says. "When I was a little girl, I knew I would be a librarian—not because I wasn't popular or athletic, because I was both those things. I loved books I liked and I loved books I hated. I got my first library card when I was six. By the time I was eight, my mother took all the restrictions off that card. She would have taken them off earlier, but she didn't know they were there. I learned things from the characters of Dr. Seuss, Harper Lee, Kurt Vonnegut, and Alice Walker. I have never read a book that didn't enrich me. Even a bad book taught me something about storytelling. I simply can't remember a bad experience with a book."

The Reverend Tarter shakes his head. There is unrest among the members of his congregation, who are seated together not far from the speakers.

"*Warren Peece* has gotten wonderful responses from many of the kids who were reading it," Ms. Lloyd goes on. "When given the choice to read something else in its place, not one student took the option. There was lively discussion. Kids who don't read were reading or having the book read to them, exactly the response any good teacher would normally die to have. I sent home a permission slip, was more than willing to let parents who may have been offended by the language or the issues have their student read an alternate book. Not one did, until this challenge. It seems fine to me for any parent to object to a book and have his or her child read something else. It seems un-American to let that parent tell the school district or the parents of other children what they can and should read in school."

She steps back from the table and turns to face the audience full on.

A man named Jeremy Godfrey rises from the middle of the Red Brickers. He doesn't know his son sat through the furnace-room readings. "Ms. Lloyd," he says. "I don't for one minute doubt your dedication to the kids or to books, but you're simply wrong on this one. We had one of our best students, a boy in your class, read the book and critique it on issues and language, and I for one simply cannot see how you think it's healthy for our kids to be reading this garbage—and I don't use that term lightly—when there are so many good books out there. For the life of me, I don't know why you chose that book, or any of Mr. Crutcher's books, for that matter. His positions are so clearly biased. Why didn't you choose something less controversial?"

"Because your kids won't read less controversial books," Ms. Lloyd says back.

"You are a teacher," he says. "It's your job to require our kids to read them."

"You are offering me a solution that makes kids hate to read, Mr. Godfrey, and that is simply not acceptable."

"What they read is just as important as *that* they read."

"That's absurd. Reading is the door to learning."

Another voice says, "Once we allow evil into our minds, it's impossible to eradicate it. We're against this book because it is irresponsible."

Another says, "I can't believe an employee of the school knows so little about our kids that she would not pay attention to the kind of filth that is out there today. We can't stop it from being written, but we can stop it from infiltrating our schools. This is a perfect example of why we need to be vigilant."

Several students laugh loudly, call taunts.

Things start to get a bit ugly then, and Mr. Northcutt pounds his gavel to restore order, threatening to clear the room or end the meeting if people don't calm down.

I notice Montana West is not present to represent the furnace-room kids, and it takes me less than a minimillimicrosecond to find her three blocks away, wrapping up the homework her father told her she had to finish before she leaves the house. She rushes toward her car, which she has been forbidden to drive until she "straightens up." She must be straightened, 'cause she's planning on getting in.

At the Legion Hall, person after person steps to the mike, calling alternately for decency or intellectual freedom. I can't help wishing Eddie were here to see what he started yesterday.

Chad Nash steps up. The audience waits, hears his nervous breathing into the mike, his mouth is so close. And he says it. "I'm gay," he says. To a person, the YFC kids go wide-eyed. "And I'm a member of YFC. I'm so scared I can't see straight, because I believe in God and I don't want to go to hell, but I don't want to live the rest of my life this scared. There is a character in the book who is also gay. When I read about him, I felt better. It was the first time in my life I ever read about a gay person being brave, except for the guy on 9/11 who helped bring the airplane down before it hit the Capitol building. I read *Warren Peece* and I felt *hope.* And then they took it away because of the very thing that I thought made it good. I feel awful right now because I know everybody is going to hate me." His gaze darts until it falls on the YFC group. "But I'm glad I said it, because I'd rather have you hate me than hold this secret inside me anymore." He stands a little longer, looking confused. "I guess I better go now."

The meeting approaches two hours in length. Kids support Chad Nash; kids condemn him. A kid from the furnace room says *Warren Peece* is the only book he ever read; a kid from YFC says it's the most disgusting book he ever read. A kid from the furnace room says the kid from YFC didn't read it because it got constipated. The kid from YFC says that's confiscated, you moron. Northcutt brings down the gavel on comments like that again and again.

Since I can be all places at once, I see my father at the back of the room, glancing at his watch, at the same time I see Eddie Proffit crouching in an orderly's closet about fifteen feet from his room in the county hospital, waiting for the hall to clear so he can sprint to his escape. My man Eddie is not going to miss this meeting and the great surprise just because he's crazy. He's been in the closet almost forty-five minutes, and each time he starts for the door another hospital employee appears in the hall. Suddenly all is clear, and he scurries to the exit, slides out unseen, and runs toward the American Legion Hall, just under three miles away.

A red Saturn pulls into the American Legion Hall parking lot when Eddie is still a mile away. My dad sees the headlights through the rear window and quietly moves to the door to greet his invited guest.

"Calvin Bartholomew," he says, extending his hand.

"Chris Crutcher," the stranger says, gripping it.

"Glad you could make it," Dad says.

"I think I am, too," Crutcher says. "How bad is it?"

"About what you'd expect," Dad says.

Crutcher says, "That bad. Is the Proffit boy here to introduce me?"

Dad shakes his head. "Long story, but he's in the county hospital awaiting a psychological evaluation."

"I won't even guess how that came about."

Dad smiles. "They're prescribing an exorcism."

The two step into the back of the room and remain standing, unnoticed. "We'll let them talk a while longer, and when the board president calls for an end to public testimony, I'll introduce you."

"Sounds good."

The crowd is intimidating. Crutcher speaks before large groups often enough, but is usually invited by people who pay him, which, he believes, means they want to hear what he has to say. Though he has been challenged and even banned before, he has never sat through a meeting where so many people came right out and called him evil. It works in his favor, though, because he feels a righteous anger rising, and he has the element of surprise.

When the line has dwindled, Mr. Tarter gets up. "I've been in this community more than twenty years," he says, smiling and nodding to the crowd, "both as a teacher and a pastor. I may have as much investment in your town and your schools as anyone in this room."

Nods from the members of his church, not so many from others, though many nonmembers believe they owe a great debt to Sanford Tarter. He is hard-nosed when it comes to discipline, but few students pass through his classroom without becoming competent in the written and spoken language. To say the least he is a formidable force.

"I have nothing but respect for Ruth Lloyd. She has been a valuable resource to me and other members of the faculty, and she is a tireless advocate for kids and for literacy. But this isn't about that. In an era of school shootings and declining family values and teachers being handcuffed from using tried-and-true disciplinary techniques, in this era of drugs and immoral behavior, the stakes are way too high. The characters in Chris Crutcher's books are disrespectful in their speech and in their actions. They are willful and to a great extent are left on their own to make decisions way too important for adolescents to make, again, particularly in light of our current culture. Either we protect our children and our values, or we don't. I for one think *this* is the place we start. Certainly Crutcher's book isn't the worst; it's simply the one that brought this problem to our attention. The truth is, I believe his stories are irrelevant and only marginally well written. The important factor is, Bear Creek, Idaho, can go against national trends and reclaim our pride. I think we can be a beacon to the rest of the country, set an example of decency.

"As a teacher and pastor, I understand the meaning of separation of church and state, and the material in this book is appropriate for neither.

"I have said before, and I say again, having been to the man's website, that his true agenda may very well be homosexuality. Homosexuality in this book and in several others he's written is treated as if it's as common as a rash. You just heard the testimony of a boy who now feels the decision to be homosexual is okay. Enough said. I'm about to call for a vote here, and I hope this school board, as it represents the community, will use common sense."

The back door bangs open, and my tenacious buddy, soaked in sweat from running three miles at state cross-country-meet speed, stands backed by the porch light. He brushes past my dad, stops to ask Chris Crutcher if he's Chris Crutcher, is delighted to discover he is, and strides to the microphone.

The crowd is nearly dumbstruck. Though roughly fifty percent of them already understand the meaning of "surreal," they'll *all* know it after tonight. They thought my boy Eddie was safely socked away.

"Hey," he says. "I'll make this quick, because I have a feeling the night guys at the loony bin have already discovered the pillows under my covers aren't me, so they'll be here with nets in a minute. Two things: When I was out of my mind with fear because I kept seeing dead people all over the place, Mr. Tarter told me probably God was scaring me into being good, which meant scaring me into getting baptized. He and the Youth for Christ kids tried to get me to hurry up so I could join them here tonight and fight for getting rid of this book. But I was a bad guy, like a spy. I want everybody to know Mr. Tarter is the one behind all this. He told us in the youth group that he couldn't get directly involved because of the two hats he wears. I guess that's legal and everything, but it's kind of deceptive, which teachers and preachers aren't supposed to be. Anyway, I read *Warren Peece* when I was feeling so alone I could barely breathe. I found friends there. They weren't as good as having my friend Billy B., but Billy B. is gone and my dad is gone, and my friends in this book stood in pretty good. Wanna know why? Of course you do. Because they felt as alone as I did. When I heard somebody wanted the book banned, it almost felt like one more friend was dying, and I couldn't stand that, so I turned myself into a spy to see if I could stop them. But I couldn't. They're too strong. Billy B.'s dad actually got fired from the school for reading to the kids who didn't read very well and the ones who couldn't afford to get the book on Amazon.com and finish it. A guy who works at the school got fired for firing kids up to read. Life gets 'curiouser and curiouser.' I got that from a book.

"Anyway, I decided to do what Mr. Tarter said and go to Chris Crutcher's website, and guess what

I found. I found Chris Crutcher, and he lives only about a hundred miles from here. And guess what else? His phone number is right there on the website. So I called him up. And guess what else else? He came. So I'm not going to talk anymore and get myself put away again. I'm going to let him talk. Please welcome the author of *Warren Peece* and many other good books with bad words—Chris Crutcher."

Almost in unison, the crowd turns to see Crutcher walking down the aisle.

"And by the way," Eddie says. "I know I'm not Jesus."

17

First-Name Basis

"Good evening. I appreciate your allowing me to be here tonight and giving me this time."

Maxwell West stands. "Point of order, Mr. Chairman. Mr. Crutcher is not on our list of speakers. We have spent more than enough time to make a decision, and he clearly has an agenda."

"Come on, West. Let the man talk. He drove a hundred miles; you want him to see us as inhospitable? He doesn't have any more of an agenda than you do." It's Robert McMaster, a logger who has been silent all evening. His words meet with general agreement.

But Mr. Northcutt comes down on Mr. West's side, citing his point of order as being valid.

The back door swings open again, and Montana West storms down the aisle toward the mike looking like Rosemary's teenager. She's wearing so much black and silver she could be mistaken for an Oakland Raider. Black skirt, black T-shirt with LEVITICUS SUCKS emblazoned in shiny silver across the chest, black boots. Every hole in her body not put there by the universe is plugged with silver jewelry, and she wears spiked wrist and ankle bands. She carries a black notebook right up to the microphone, brushing past Chris Crutcher. "Excuse me," she says, and lowers the mike to her level. "I'm sorry, Mr. Chairman, I was supposed to deliver the pro-*Warren Peece* presentation, but my dad wouldn't let me out of the house until my homework was finished."

She takes papers from the notebook and hands them to her father. "All done, Daddy. Check it for me, will you?"

Maxwell West does not take the papers.

"Young lady," Mr. Northcutt says, "that shirt is totally inappropriate for these proceedings. I cannot—"

"You're right," Montana says. "But my chest isn't big enough for 'Mr. Tarter's Red Brick Church' or 'The Bear Creek School Board,' so I had to settle for 'Leviticus.'"

"I can't allow you to wear it here."

Montana crosses her arms over her torso, with both hands gripping the lower hem of the shirt. "If you insist," she says, and starts to pull it off.

"NO!" Maxwell yells. "DON'T YOU DARE, YOUNG LADY."

She lets the shirt fall back. "Jeez. Make up your mind." Montana takes out several pieces of paper from the notebook and holds them open in front of the microphone. "One out of three girls is sexually abused," she says, reading from the paper. "One out of five boys. The statistics on both boys and girls who are emotionally or physically abused are hard to zero in on because of definition, but understand that if you're in a class of twenty-five kids, there are several. Approximately one in ten humans is gay. Anywhere from twenty to sixty-five percent of the students in a high-school classroom are sexually active in some way; could be higher. Every class has at least one kid who's anorexic or bulimic and one who cuts herself or himself. I'm one of those. I cut on myself because it's pain I can control, instead of pain from you-know-where from you-know-who that I *can't* control. When I feel like I have no control, I get it wherever I can. When you try to control what we think, we feel out of control. We think you're cowards when you won't talk with us."

"Montana, this is not the time or the place for this. I'm asking you to step away from that microphone. We'll talk about this at home."

"You kidding?" she says. "You know how long I'm going to be grounded for this?" Then, "Of course you do."

She turns back to the crowd. "Those are some of the issues that get talked about in *Warren Peece*. Can't give you the statistics on drug and alcohol use in our school, but it's safe to say there isn't a teenager in this room who doesn't know at least three kids who are in trouble. Mr. Tarter, and the rest of you teachers, too: The next time you stand in front of your classroom, give yourself a moment of silence, look around the room, and do the math. Ask yourself if you have the ba—the courage to talk to us about them."

She stares at the section with the most teachers, adjusts the mike. "I read the book. I was pushed for time when it was assigned, and I was going to scam it; you know, read a little and pry the rest out of my friends or Ms. Lloyd, and slide with a B. But then you guys tried to censor it, so I read every word. Twice.

"It was a pretty good book. I've read better. But what was way cool was that a bunch of kids I like liked it way more than I did. They started talking about the issues and the characters and all the things teachers say they want us to talk about in regard to a book. You need to understand—some of my friends have never read a book cover to cover; I have friends who take pride in being ignorant. But they read this book and they liked it, and that's all anyone should have to say."

The room is silent. Crutcher stands off to the side, trying to read the faces in the crowd. Eddie nods and pumps his fist slightly. He really wishes this girl would fall in love with him just so he could be seen with her. I wish she would, too.

Montana recognizes Chris Crutcher from his picture on the back flap, registers just a hint of surprise, and regroups. "Mr. Crutcher seems to be standing right here, and I don't know whether or not he has the guts to talk to us about those things, but I do know he has the guts to write about them and that's more than we get from you most of the time. Thank you, Mr. Crutcher. And if I'd known you were here I wouldn't have said, 'I've read better.'"

Crutcher smiles. "You can call me Chris."

"If you don't want to lose us," Montana says to the crowd, "stop trying to tell us how to think. It makes it almost impossible to respect you." She squints her eyes at the board. "I know we don't have a prayer to stop the banning of this book, because I know how many of you are Red Brickers. So go ahead. Take it. We'll find it and read it, and we'll post a list at the city library of every book you ban and read every one of them. We'll carry them, front cover out, all over campus, and we'll talk about them, loud, with one another."

Montana starts to walk away and quickly turns back. "And if you don't let Mr. Crutcher talk, you are nothing but cowards."

Montana walks down the aisle to huge applause.

Crutcher stands next to the microphone, unsettled because he doesn't know protocol, whether to talk or wait for permission. He takes his cue from Montana West.

"Tell you what," he says. "You don't have to let me talk. I don't have anything to say that could come close in accuracy to what you just heard. So my presentation is this." He points to Montana as she walks out the back door. "What she said."

Within a half hour, Crutcher is sitting in a local coffee shop with Ms. Lloyd and Dad and my good friend Eddie Proffit, who has miraculously been spared by the owners of the booby hatch.

By the time they get their second cup of coffee, *Warren Peece* and the rest of Crutcher's books have been removed from the shelves of the Bear Creek High School library.

18

GETTING PUBLISHED

I sit high in the stacks for the next week while the Bear Creek High School library is cleansed of Chris Crutcher, and subsequently of Alex Sanchez and Terry Davis and some of Walter Dean Myers, Judy Blume, Alice Walker, Kurt Vonnegut, Robert Cormier, Stephen King, and J.K. Rowling. It is also cleansed of Ms. Lloyd, because she can simply no longer work where there is no respect for literature. In truth, far more of the townspeople are against censorship than for, but the school board has the last say. The Reverend

Tarter and his followers were far less successful when they brought their same complaints to the city library. *That* board has not been infiltrated. Many high-school students begin using the city library almost exclusively, creating jobs for Ms. Lloyd and my dad.

Eddie Proffit has lived up to his last name, turning a handsome one (profit, I mean) on T-shirts and bumper stickers reading LEVITICUS SUCKS, though he did get a three-day vacation and had to come up with a written apology for wearing the prototype T-shirt, which he borrowed from Montana West, to school. He's offered Montana a fifty-percent cut. They're working out the details. His written apology was long and rambling and hardly an apology at all, but since it came with a promise not to wear the T-shirt to school anymore, he is reinstated.

I'm ready to go. Eddie has his feet on the ground, is running like a champ and filling his life with new friends (he's even edging toward Montana West with lust in his heart), many of them the kinds of friends most people warn their kids away from—but the word is out that he might be Jesus, and he has attained antihero status among kids who wear Montana's colors. Our next run will be my last. He'll ask me to stay, and I'll say he knows everything he needs to know now and I'll just be in the way. He'll beg me, I'll tell him okay, I'll stay until he gives me permission to leave, and the moment he knows he's in control, he'll let me go. I'm not predicting the future; I just know my friend.

As I look back over this story, I believe more than ever it ought to be part of the stable of banned literature at Bear Creek High School, though I have been careful not to take the name of the universe in vain or use bodily or sexual functions as verbs or adjectives. The content alone will get the job done.

I can't get it published under the name of Billy Bartholomew, because he's just another dead white guy, but I can say all I know about what it's like being dead and not alter world philosophy one bit if I put it under Chris Crutcher's authorship. I mean, who's going to believe *he* has the inside intellectual track on anything? The vast majority of the world's readership doesn't know who he is. When I burrowed into his mind to catch up on his books, I found him mired in the quicksand of writer's block. He hasn't completed anything in more than two years, and though his editor is a picture of patience on the outside, she's wondering if he's run out of stories. So I will this story into his Word files, but at twenty-one grams, I can't find a way to hit the *send* icon. I take it back out and pop it into his editor's computer under his name.

Imagine how surprised Chris Crutcher is to get *this* e-mail.

Chris,

My goodness, I didn't even know you were working on this. I made a few small changes, but I have to say it's the cleanest first draft you've ever turned in. Read my changes and get back to me. You must have had real focus. Very clever, sticking yourself into the story. You'll be famous yet.

Virginia

Crutcher reads the story, glances at the pile of Chapter One, Page Ones on the floor beneath his keyboard, recognizes this as similar to the ploy he used to get through high school, and fires off an e-mail.

Virginia,

What did you think I was doing? Sitting on my skinny—

I promised not to use those words in my story.

Chris

Good-bye, Eddie Proffit, Dad, Ms. Lloyd, Chris Crutcher. I'm off to explore newly formed galaxies and black holes and experience the breathtaking power and grace of the universe. I'll bump against all of you soon. You probably sooner than the others, Chris Crutcher.